HOLIDAY BLUES

"Your father and I have decided to get a divorce," Denise announced and watched the shock spread around the table. For the first time Aunt Etta actually appeared at a loss for words. Uncle Eddie looked at his nephew as if expecting him to say it was all a joke.

Anthony simply stared at his mother as if he couldn't get his mind to reconcile with what she'd just said. Christine had no such difficulty. She was as volatile in her reaction as Denise had expected.

"Mama, Daddy, what were you thinking?" Christine cried. "You're ruining the holidays for all of us!"

Denise stared at the accusing faces and rose regally to her feet. "I've spent the past twenty-seven years giving to everyone except myself. . . . Well, I suggest you make other arrangements." She tossed her napkin on the table. "The queen is abdicating her throne."

Donna   Francis
Hill   &   Ray

Rockin' Around That Christmas Tree

St. Martin's Paperbacks

ROCKIN' AROUND THAT CHRISTMAS TREE

Copyright © 2003 by Donna Hill and Francis Ray.
Excerpt from *Getting Hers* copyright © 2004 by Donna Hill.
Excerpt from *You and No Other* copyright © 2004 by Francis Ray.

All rights reserved. No part of this book may be used or reproduced in any manner whatsoever without written permission except in the case of brief quotations embodied in critical articles or reviews. For information address St. Martin's Press, 175 Fifth Avenue, New York, NY 10010.

Library of Congress Catalog Card Number: 2003047167

ISBN: 0-312-99363-3
EAN: 80312-99363-4

Printed in the United States of America

St. Martin's Press hardcover edition / November 2003
St. Martin's Paperbacks edition / November 2004

St. Martin's Paperbacks are published by St. Martin's Press, 175 Fifth Avenue, New York, NY 10010.

10 9 8 7 6 5 4 3 2 1

We lovingly dedicate this book to all of our loyal fans who have supported us through the years, and welcome the new ones. May your holiday season and all the days that follow bring you joy, peace, and happiness.

We deeply thank our ever-creative editor, Monique Patterson, who told us we could do this, believed in us, and made sure we got this done! To the best agents a writer could have, Manie Barron and Pattie Steele-Perkins, for guiding us and keeping our hectic lives in order.

Denise's Tea Cakes

2 cups sugar
¾ cup solid shortening
½ cup buttermilk
2 eggs
1 teaspoon baking soda
1 teaspoon vanilla extract
2–3 cups sifted flour

Cream sugar and solid shortening in a large mixing bowl. Add eggs and stir until smooth. Combine baking soda with ¼ cup flour, then add to ingredients in mixing bowl. Mix well. Add vanilla and stir. Alternate flour and buttermilk until buttermilk is gone. Continue with flour until dough is firm. Cover bowl with waxed paper and refrigerate for 3–4 hours. Roll out dough, cut into desired shapes. Bake at 375 degrees for 8–12 minutes (depending on thickness of cookie). Lift with spatula onto cooling rack. Or just eat hot. Enjoy.

One

Denise Morrison could have cheerfully strangled her husband, Edward, a man she'd loved for more than half her life. *Enough was enough.* Minutes earlier she'd been elbow deep in dishwater and he'd asked her to refill his coffee cup while he leisurely read the *Atlanta Journal* newspaper before going to work. The only reason he wasn't trying to wrestle her apron from around his neck was that he'd said "please."

Men! They had the sensitivity and the single-mindedness of an ant.

"Good coffee," Edward mumbled.

Denise rolled her eyes as she continued to wash the breakfast dishes. Once they'd had so much to talk about, to plan. Those days had somehow slipped by and in their place was complacency.

Denise paused to stare out the window of their rambling two-story home on an oversize lot in the

Atlanta suburbs. The large well-manicured yard was still green with rye grass in late November. The four seven-foot oak trees that they'd raised blisters on their hands to plant now towered forty feet and gave shade to the winter-hardy petunias and the hammock that hadn't been used in years. The trees and grass thrived, but their marriage had lost its magic. The knowledge hurt deep inside her. Love like theirs should have lasted a lifetime instead of twenty-seven years. They had accomplished so much and now seemed to share so little.

"I went shopping for the kids yesterday," Edward said.

Denise glanced around at Edward sitting across the room at the dining table instead of at the end of the island directly behind her. He used to sit there to be closer to her when they'd first built the house twenty years ago. She tried to remember the last time he had eaten his meal on the island while she worked in the kitchen or the last time they had sat side by side on the two stools on the end, arms and hips, hearts and minds touching, and couldn't.

"Denise, did you hear me?" Edward asked, his gaze still on the business section of the newspaper. His dark head tilted to one side to pitch his voice in her direction. She wasn't even important enough to take his attention from the newspaper.

"I heard."

He nodded and turned the page, then he put the newspaper down and swiveled toward her. His handsome chocolate-hued face was animated as always when he spoke of their two children. "I got the diamond earrings Christine has been hinting at and Anthony the newest Palm Pilot. They're wrapped, so you won't have to worry about it. We're finished with their big gifts."

For a moment Denise was at a loss as to know what to say. "I thought we were going shopping for them together?"

Edward turned back to the newspaper. "Christine called yesterday to say hello, and mentioned she had seen the earrings on sale. I didn't want them to sell out since she had her heart set on them. There was an electronics store across the street, so I decided to take care of Anthony's as well."

Denise placed the plate in the drying rack and reached for the skillet. He took care of too many things. The sad thing was, he wasn't doing it maliciously. He'd been brought up to take care of his family. He was, in her grandmother's words, a man's man.

"It will be great having them home for Thanksgiving," he continued. "Aunt Etta and Uncle Eddie will be here too. I left you some extra money on the dresser to get anything you need. I want the dinner to be the best ever. This will be the first Thanksgiving with the children here since Christine got married and Anthony moved into his own place."

Denise's slim fingers tightened around the skillet handle. So, now she was needed! She could cook for the family, but her help wasn't needed to help pick out her own children's Christmas presents. For one crazy moment she thought of seeing if the skillet could sail like a Frisbee. "I went grocery shopping last week," she said evenly, keeping her temper in check.

"Good." He stood, shoving the ladder-backed chair beneath the round oak table. "And another thing, you know I don't like you sewing for other people. I hope that wedding dress you were working on last night is the end of it."

She spun around. Dishwater dripped from her hands onto the spotless hardwood floor. Sewing was the only thing she did that was strictly *her* accomplishment. "I like sewing. People are beginning to call me."

He paused in pulling on his black baseball cap with the name of his construction company emblazoned in gold lettering. "I hope you told them no. You have a family and a house to care for. And you certainly don't need the money."

I need to be needed, she almost said. "Is it so bad that I want to earn my own money, to want to be able to buy you or the children something without first going to you?"

Impatient lines radiated across Edward's strong forehead. "I take care of my family, Denise. If you need money, all you have to do is ask or write a check."

"I'd rather have my own," she said with an unconscious tilt of her chin.

"It *is* your money," he told her with a brisk jerk of his baseball cap. "I can't see why you'd think otherwise. Have I ever said anything about how you spend money or asked you about a check you'd written?"

"No, but you write the checks for all the bills and the expenses."

"So you won't have to worry about it," he told her. "I do it for you."

She shook her head. "But remember how I wanted to buy a new sewing machine after people started asking me about making clothes for them, when they saw how beautiful the dresses I designed and made for Christine and her wedding attendants were? You said no."

"You shouldn't be sewing for people. They just want to get it cheap because they know you won't charge them full price," he said, picking up the insulated lunch Thermos she always prepared for him when he planned to work in his office.

"That may be true, but it also gives me the chance to do something I love," she said, trying to make him understand. "You and the children certainly don't need me sewing for you. I completely redid the house before the wedding. Sewing helps fill the day."

"With the holidays coming, you'll be busy enough," he said, a hint of exasperation in his deep voice. "I don't want my wife sewing for people and being taken advantage of."

Edward had always had enough pride for two men and was more stubborn than a mule when he'd made up his mind. "They're not taking advantage of me," Denise replied. "I get the pleasure out of seeing my ideas come alive, and they get a beautiful dress. The customer and I both win."

His brown eyes narrowed. "If you want to sew, then sew for yourself or Aunt Etta."

"Neither one of us needs a wedding gown nor any of the other designs I've been thinking about lately," she told him, her hands pressed against the cool ceramic tile on top of the island, trying to tease him back into his usual good humor. It didn't work. His mouth remained in a thin, disapproving line.

Unwilling to give up, she tried another tack. "Sewing makes me feel the same way you feel when a design for one of your projects is finished."

He tsked dismissively. "You can't compare what we do."

Denise realized it would be useless to continue. He didn't think what she did was important. She looked at him and wanted to snatch the lunch Thermos out of his hand. He was almost a stranger. He used to listen to her, even if he always made the final decision. Perhaps it was her fault for always being a follower instead of being more assertive. If she had been, perhaps he would treat her as an equal in their marriage.

"What am I supposed to do with my time while your behind is glued to that ugly orange chair watching TV?" she asked with growing irritation. Not for love or money would he let her get rid of or reupholster the bulky lounger that was covered with an atrocious bright orange tweed. "We haven't gone out to dinner or to a movie in months."

"My chair is not ugly and I'm tired when I get home. I've never forced or stopped you from doing anything, have I?" he challenged.

"No, but you made it so obvious that you didn't want me to do it that I felt uncomfortable."

He gave the baseball cap another impatient jerk. "I'm just trying to look out for your best interests. You didn't come up as rough as I did. You don't know how harsh the world can be, and I don't intend for you to find out. You have a nice home, all the bills are paid, a new car. I work hard to give you everything you want."

Everything, but the freedom to make my own decisions and run my own life, she thought silently. She was no longer a teenage bride, unsure of herself and looking to him for guidance and approval. She was a grown woman who needed to live her own life and make her own mistakes if necessary.

"Denise."

The unyielding way he said her name was a command for her to fall in line as always. She could argue, but she'd promised herself long ago that she'd never get into the screaming matches her parents had while she was growing up. Edward wasn't being mean, he was just doing as he always had, taking care of his family by handling all the finances and solving all the problems. He didn't seem to understand that his making all the important decisions made her feel like a bystander in her own home.

Her shoulders slumped, and when she spoke her voice was barely above a whisper. "All right, Edward."

He nodded his head in satisfaction. "If you get any more calls about sewing, just tell them no. You'll be too busy preparing for the holidays. I'll start putting up the Christmas lights tonight so Anthony can throw the switch after Thanksgiving dinner." He stuck the business section of the newspaper under his arm. "I won't be home until late. Good-bye."

Denise watched him walk out of the kitchen toward the front of the house where his SUV was parked. No good-bye kiss, no hug, nothing, just instructions to make Thanksgiving dinner the best ever and not to sew for anyone. She had the childish urge to stick her tongue out at his broad back. She was his wife, not his housekeeper.

It used to be that they couldn't be in the same room without touching. Now they seldom touched unless it was in bed and then they'd burn up the sheets. But she needed—wanted—that same loving feeling when her feet were planted firmly on the floor. Her mouth quirked as she thought, *With my clothes on*.

They'd met when she was seventeen and he'd come as a carpenter's helper to repair her grandmother's wooden back porch. She'd answered the door, seen Edward with a two-by-four on his broad shoulder, and fallen hard. Deeply muscled and lean-hipped, he'd made her body shiver and her heart pound.

She'd made excuses to go outside while he was working. No matter how busy he was he always stopped to get the back screen door for her. She'd heard the other worker teasing him, but he hadn't seemed to mind. That night he had called and they'd

started going out. For her there had never been anyone else.

Their closeness was cemented even more when
he helped her during her parents' messy divorce.
After years of making each other and everyone
around them miserable, her parents had finally decided to move on. Denise had been sent to Atlanta to
live with her maternal grandmother because her
mother worked at night and her father was moving
to another city. She had looked at the move as a
punishment until she'd met Edward.

Walking over to the table, she picked up his coffee cup and took it back to the sink. He had always
been so sure of himself, so assertive. Since she had
lacked those qualities, she had admired them in him.
But Edward had to accept that she was capable of
making her own decisions, of running her life. She
desperately wanted to do both.

The phone on the counter rang and she picked up
the receiver without much enthusiasm. "Hello."

"Good morning, Mama."

A smile blossomed on Denise's face on hearing
her daughter and oldest child's voice. "Good morning, Christine. How's Reese?" The happy laughter
she usually heard when she mentioned her daughter's husband of five months didn't materialize. A
frown worked its way across Denise's brow. "Is
everything all right?"

"Sure, Mama," Christine quickly said, but the words sounded forced. "It's just that since Reese started his second-year residency at the hospital he's been spending a lot of extra hours there. I miss him."

Denise tried to relax, but couldn't. If there was a problem, would her daughter tell her? Both Christine and her brother, Anthony, sought the counsel of their father more than hers. Another area over which Edward thought he should have dominion.

Christine bubbled over with life and the men she'd dated were usually the same way. Denise had been surprised when she first met Reese, a first-year surgical resident at Atlanta General. He was a tall, lean, good-looking young man with a serious face and a disposition to match. They'd met when Christine, a social worker for the city, had gone to the hospital to visit a child in her caseload and Reese had been the attending physician. "All marriages go through a period of adjustment. Reese is a wonderful man and he loves you," Denise said.

"I know. Is Daddy around?"

"No, he just left. Can I help?"

"Thanks, but I need to talk with him."

Denise tapped her fingernails on the countertop. "If it's about the furniture you and Reese have stored in the garage, it's not in the way."

"It's not that. Daddy already said we could leave

it there until we decide what we want to do with it," Christine told her, sounding a bit distracted.

Denise might have known. Daddy had decided, therefore the opinion of her mother didn't matter. She continued to tap out an agitated tattoo. *Typical*, she thought. *Just typical*.

"I gotta run. 'Bye, Mama. I'll see you in a couple of days for Thanksgiving. I can't wait for some of your broccoli and cheese casserole." She smacked her lips.

"Hmm," Denise murmured. She could cook, but not help with anything else.

"We're going to see Reese's parents this weekend," Christine continued, unaware of her mother's growing irritation. "She's a terrible cook." Christine giggled. "Even Reese says so, but she's a wonderful woman."

Denise couldn't recall Christine ever calling her wonderful except in terms of her cooking or sewing. Her initial happy mood on hearing her daughter's voice declined sharply. She knew she had to get off the phone before it came through in her voice. "The roads will be heavy with holiday traffic. You two drive carefully."

"We will. 'Bye, Mama."

Denise hung up the phone. For a long moment her hand stayed on the receiver as she tried to push away the recurring thoughts that had plagued her these past months. Her family loved her, but they didn't need her.

She looked around the bright lemon yellow kitchen with blue accents. The yellow ceramic tile on the countertop gleamed, as did the hardwood floor extending to the family room to her right. A competent housekeeper could replace her and no one would probably notice.

Tired of her own unhappy thoughts, Denise made her way out of the kitchen, up the stairs to the second floor, then farther to the attic. The large room was as scrupulously clean as the rest of the house. In the very center beneath track lighting and between two elongated windows was her grandmother's old Singer sewing machine on which Denise had learned to sew and continued to use. A few feet away was the scarred oak kitchen table upon which she and her grandmother had shared so many wonderful meals and good times. The table was now used as a cutting surface for Denise's designs.

Usually, when she was in this room, along with her grandmother's two most prized possessions, Denise felt her nearness and her unconditional love. Today was different. She felt every one of her forty-five years, and then some. She felt old and tired; even worse, useless.

On a dress mannequin was the wedding gown she

was sewing for the daughter of a friend. The young woman and her mother had been by yesterday for her final fitting and were scheduled to pick up the dress that afternoon. The bride-to-be had glowed with happiness.

Denise absently fingered the floor-length skirt of heavy white satin. People had said the same thing about her when her wedding day approached. She had just finished high school and Edward had completed his freshman year at Grambling. Neither wanted to wait to get married. They couldn't keep their hands off each other and had been so in love, so sure of themselves and their happily ever after.

When had the glow begun to dim?

Was it when Edward had to drop out his junior year to get a full-time job after her unplanned pregnancy with Christine? Or was it her planned, but complicated, pregnancy with Anthony, a math wizard, two years later? Or had it begun later when Edward's construction business started taking off and he was more and more often gone from home?

Or did the cause really matter? The outcome was the same. The magic was gone from their marriage. That thought brought a pang to Denise's heart and carried her to the old trunk on the other side of the attic.

Kneeling, Denise lifted the lid. Inside were the

treasured quilts her grandmother had sewn by hand, the first dress Denise had made by herself, the table linen for the first tiny apartment she and Edward shared, Christine and Anthony's christening gowns. So many warm memories were wrapped carefully in tissue paper, and that was exactly where her life would remain if she let things continue the way they were.

Edward saw her as a wife and mother, not as the independent woman and partner to him she yearned to be. Part of the problem, she knew, was that the few jobs she'd held before she became pregnant with Christine were a way of making ends meet and had nothing to do with establishing a career. After her daughter was born, Denise had never gone back to work. Taking care of her family became her focus and goal in life.

But now that her children were grown and Edward was successful, she had begun to think about how she might focus her time and energy. After receiving so many compliments on Christine's and her attendants' dresses, Denise had realized what she wanted to do.

Only Edward refused to listen. He knew very well other women had successful, fulfilling lives outside the home, but he wanted her chained to the house with a spatula in one hand and a vacuum cleaner in the other. Even their daughter had a career she enjoyed and could look at what she did with pride.

Edward might not see her sewing as measuring up to what he did, but Denise did. She loved Edward, but she didn't want to continue going through the motions of marriage. She wanted the juice, the fire, back in their marriage; she wanted what they'd shared when they were crazy in love and stood side by side.

Edward needed a wake-up call. He needed to understand that he couldn't run her life or take her for granted. If she thought the knothead didn't love her, she'd have packed his bag and sent him to live with his eccentric aunt and uncle. That would get his attention.

She paused as the thought swirled around in her head. What if he really thought she wanted out of their marriage? Would it shock him enough to make him really listen to what she was saying? She swallowed. Was she courageous enough to jeopardize her marriage? Despite everything, she loved Edward and couldn't imagine life without him.

Her teeth clamped down on her bottom lip. She'd never been a gambler, but did she have a choice if she wanted Edward to see her as a partner and not as a cook and housekeeper, if she wanted their marriage to be what it had once been?

Her arms drew the quilts and christening gowns to her chest. She really *didn't* have a choice. Tonight, when Edward came home, she was going to shake things up. She was going to ask for a divorce.

Two

Edward stepped outside to an unusually brisk Atlanta morning. Gazing across his lawn, then out onto the quiet tree-lined street, he smiled with pride at all that he'd accomplished.

Everyone in this upper-middle-class development was a blend of old family money and new economics—those who'd made their mark during the wave of financial prosperity in the eighties. His neighbors owned their two cars and their homes, and their children all went to "good schools." Husbands went to work every day, some of them owning their businesses. They made the money that paid for the houses, the cars, the manicured lawns, and the "better" education. The wives took care of the family. *She* was the thread that held everything together in the home. And they certainly didn't take in "day work" to make ends meet or to fill some need.

"Hey, Jeff. How's it going?" Edward called out to his neighbor next door.

"Wife's due any minute now," he said with a chuckle. "Have to put in some extra time at the office."

"I hear ya. Take it easy," Edward said as Jeff hopped behind the wheel of his Benz and pulled out of his driveway.

Edward pulled up the collar of his jacket as a cold breeze slid around his neck and down his back. He took a quick look at the overcast sky. "Rain," he muttered as he quickly slid into his Escalade and revved the engine.

He'd come a long way from the poverty, illiteracy, and family strife of his early days in Alabama, he mused as he glided by the photo-perfect homes along Morningside Lane. He'd seen up close what working on one's hands and knees had done to his mother. He'd witnessed the shame and regret that etched permanent lines of sorrow on his father's weather-beaten face because he couldn't support his family, and the total exhaustion that turned down the corners of his mother's mouth and curved her back. Then one day his father just couldn't take it anymore, couldn't take looking at himself in the mirror and not seeing the man he believed he should be. Rather than be a burden, yet another mouth to feed, he walked out one summer afternoon and never came back. His mother quietly passed away the following winter, right on the bathroom floor of her employer's home—bristle brush and a bar of lye soap in her hands.

Edward swallowed down the knot of pain that periodically rose to his throat at the memories of days gone by and flipped on the windshield wipers as the first drops splattered angrily against the glass. He'd gone to live with his Uncle Eddie and Aunt Etta in Marietta, Georgia, until he graduated from high school. They'd done their best by him, but they were not much better off than his folks had been. They had plenty of love to give, but not much else. The life he'd lived as a boy was not what he wanted for his family. Not one day would they have to do without or see him as being less than a man, a provider, someone they would be proud to call Dad. When he lucked out and secured an athletic scholarship to Grambling, he made a vow that he would never see his family struggle or want for anything. They would be looked up to and not down on by their neighbors. And whatever it took to make that happen he would do, even if it meant saying no to his wife.

Edward reached for the radio dial and tuned into his favorite jazz station. "Body and Soul," one of his favorite John Coltrane tunes, filled the confines of the plush leather interior. He smiled. *Body and soul,* that's what his wife was to him. He knew he didn't always tell her how much she meant to him, but he tried to show her with the things he did for her and the kids. He wanted her to always know that she could depend on him, no matter what.

He eased into the turning lane and made the quick left that would take him to his office. He could see the sign from the expressway—MORRISON DESIGN AND CONSTRUCTION. Yeah, it was all his. He'd built his business from a little storefront with a desk and four chairs to a two-story, 8,000-square-foot spread with a staff of twenty.

Edward pulled into the parking lot and eased into the space marked RESERVED/OWNER. Although the front door was mere feet away, he was in for a drenching. The rain was coming down in blinding sheets by the time he'd turned off the ignition. As he jogged to the entrance, he seriously contemplated adding an underground garage for days just like this one.

"'Morning, Mr. Morrison," he heard one after another say as he double-stepped down the corridor, anxious to get out of his wet clothes. He smiled and waved along the way. He had to admit, he had a great staff, some of the most talented contractors and designers in the state. It wasn't luck and it wasn't affirmative action that landed his team one major development job after another—it was talent.

It was drive. It was pride in what they did, and it was a willingness to be the best.

"Hey, Ed, look a little wet there, brotha," William Henry said with a chuckle as he caught up with Edward moments before he entered his office.

"I'm seriously thinking about underground parking," Edward said as he took off his jacket and shook it like a wet dog. He hung it up on the hook behind his door, then looked down at his pants and wondered if Denise had remembered to have his extra work pants delivered from the cleaners. "What's up, man? Everything cool with the Davidson project?" he asked as he opened the closet on the far wall and found his slacks hanging neatly beneath plastic. He smiled. *Denise*.

"Yeah, yeah," William said, nodding as he took a seat. "I just wanted to run some things by you before we signed off on the shopping complex blueprints."

"Sure. Can you hang on a minute? Let me get out of these wet pants."

William nodded and began looking over his notes while Edward stepped into the adjoining bathroom—which was only a toilet and sink—and changed his slacks. Refreshed and dry, he stepped out and pulled up a chair next to William rather than sit behind his desk. "Shoot. What's on your mind?" Edward slid on his glasses and scanned the plans and notes that William spread out on his desk.

"I was going over the schematics for the plaza level . . ."

The two men talked for nearly forty-five minutes for what could have been a ten-minute conversation, but Edward was interrupted at least a dozen times with twice as many emergencies and inquiries to respond to.

Finally, William stood. "Thanks. I'll work out the details with the suits over at Davidson and meet with our team."

"This project is too big to let anything fall between the cracks," Edward said. "It and this company have been in the papers at least once a month for the past year. Everyone has their eye on us, waiting for us to slip up so they can slide in. There is a ton of money, prestige, and manpower involved. When we pull this off—and we will—Morrison Design and Construction will be engraved on the map."

William grinned broadly. "I know, man. We won't let you down."

Edward slapped William on the back as he walked him to the door. "I know you won't."

Edward pulled in a long breath. The Davidson contract was one that designers and contractors dreamed of. It had taken hard work and long hours at the negotiating table, but he'd won the bid. Now, it was time for show and tell. He had to be on his mark and not let anything distract him from what needed to be done. One of the reasons why his company was so successful was that he prided himself at being a hands-on boss. There was nothing that went on in his company that he didn't know about, down to the last detail; from signing off on supply orders to working shoulder to shoulder pouring foundation. He would never be accused of being the kind of owner who was ignorant to what went on in his company. He was the same way at home. A man had to be responsible. That was his motto.

He took off his glasses and walked around to his desk, all set to dive into the mound of paperwork that awaited him, just as his private line rang.

"Morrison," he said by rote.

"Hey, Dad, you don't have to sound so formal," Christine said, her voice light and teasing.

A smile spread across his mouth at the sound of his daughter's voice.

"Hey, baby girl. And to what do I owe this early morning pleasure?"

"I tried to catch you at home, but Mom said you'd already left for work."

"Gotta make an honest dollar to ensure that my family lives in the style they've grown accustomed to," he joked.

"You've always taken good care of us, Daddy. No

one can ever say otherwise. And Reese is the same way."

"How is he, anyway? Hope he's not leaving you alone too much."

"He's fine. He's been putting in extra hours at the hospital with all the cutbacks, but . . . makes it up to me every chance he gets," she added, practically singing.

"Well, doll, I think that's more information than your dear old dad needs to hear." He smiled at her laughter on the other end. "So, what can I do for you? You just name it and it's yours."

"I was really calling to find out what you think would be the perfect gift for Mom. I swear she has everything. And I'm at a total loss. I'm taking the next few days off from work and I want to get my holiday shopping done."

"Hmmm. You're right about her having everything. Maybe a watch?"

"I got her a watch for her birthday, remember?"

He didn't really, but agreed anyway.

"How about something for her sewing clients? She seems to really—"

"No, forget it. Your mother and I talked about that and after she finishes this gown—which she promised she'd do—she won't be taking in work anymore."

"Really?" Christine frowned. "If you say so," she

murmured. "Anyway, I guess I will have to figure something out on my own. Have you talked to Anthony lately?"

"Not in a few days. I guess he's all tied up with his girlfriend. The last time I talked to him he said he was going to bring her for Thanksgiving dinner. So it must be serious."

"Who would have thought that Mr. Playboy would get his date card pulled?" They both laughed.

"I know what you mean. I was pretty sure Tony was going to teach courses in being a professional bachelor. But I'm glad to see that he's finally taking life seriously and settling down. Having a good woman in your life only makes you a better man," he said.

"Do you feel that way about Mom?" she asked softly.

"I wouldn't be where I am today without her. She's been in my corner from day one, taking care of you and your brother, me, the house. She's one incredible woman," he added wistfully.

"That's really nice to hear, Dad, especially when so many marriages are falling apart. I only hope that Reese and I will stay as happy as you and Mom."

"It takes two to make a marriage work. Always remember that."

"I will. Listen, I have to run. See you for Thanksgiving. Mom promised she was going to make her famous casserole and I can't wait!"

Edward laughed. "That's one thing about your Mom; she can burn, as you young folks would say."

"And so would you," she said, laughing. "Take care, Dad."

"You too, baby girl." He hung up the phone and smiled. Yes, he had a great life.

The rest of Edward's day continued at a rapid clip, with the usual amount of headaches and successes, and by six o'clock he was more than ready to head home to a good meal and a hot bath.

When he got home, the house was strangely quiet. If he didn't know better he'd swear his wife wasn't home. But that was impossible. For the past twenty-seven years of their marriage there had not been one day that he'd come in from work or from a business trip and Denise had not been there to greet him.

"Denise! I'm home." He hung up his coat and walked into the living room. "Denise!" The room was empty. He headed for the kitchen and looked around, growing more perplexed when he noticed that the stove was bare of pots and not a scent of food was in the air.

His heart started to pound. Something was wrong. He took the stairs two at a time and flung open the bedroom door, certain that he would find his wife asleep—the only reason he could come up with to explain the unexplainable.

But when he stepped inside, he found that room empty, just like the rest of the house. For several moments, he simply stood there, totally mystified. Where was Denise? He looked on the dresser for a note and found none. He checked his cell phone to see if he'd perhaps missed a message from her, and again, nothing.

He sat down on the side of the bed. His first instinct was to reach for the phone and call the police. He tried to recall all the *Law & Order* shows he'd watched. The police would want information; the last time he saw her, height, weight, what she was wearing. And suddenly, for the life of him he couldn't remember if Denise's hair was dark brown or black.

The phone rang and he nearly jumped out of his skin. He snatched it from the receiver.

"Denise!" he shouted.

"Keep your shirt on, boy, this is your Uncle Eddie. What's wrong, can't keep up with your wife?" He chuckled. "Told you a hundred times, boy, you gotta keep 'em happy like I do with your Aunt Etta and you won't have to worry about where they are. A little James Brown, some Wild Irish Rose, and good lovin' will keep a smile on their face."

"Uncle Eddie, I really can't talk to you right now."

"You tellin' me you can't make time for your old uncle, the man that used to wipe your butt and your nose?"

"Uncle Eddie, I was a teenager when I came to live with you. I really don't think you were wiping my butt or my nose."

"Humph . . . you know what I mean. And don't sass me, boy. You're not too big for a whipping. This old man still has a few good ones left in him." He coughed a smoker's cough, "You having trouble with your woman? 'Cause if you are, you've come to the right place."

Edward shook his head, not knowing whether to laugh or scream. "Everything is fine, Uncle Eddie."

"So, where's the little lady?"

"She . . . went out."

"Hmmm, really?"

"Yes, really," he said, pacing the floor as he talked and wishing his uncle would just hang up. He needed to find his wife.

"If you say so. But just remember this one thing."

"What's that, Uncle Eddie?"

"I ain't no fool. So don't be trying to fool your old uncle. Just remember that. Hang on, your Aunt Etta wants to talk to ya."

"Uncle . . ."

"Etta! Etta! Come talk to this boy. Sounds like he can't find his wife."

Edward rolled his eyes to the heavens. He knew his aunt and uncle meant well, but they drove him crazy. Nutty as fruitcakes, his son Anthony always joked.

"Well, where in the dickens did he lose her?" Etta was saying as she came to the phone. "What you do to that woman?" Etta demanded of her nephew. "Did you run her off with those James Brown records your uncle gave you? Eddie, I told you not to give that boy those records. They done drove Denise right out of that pretty house. How come you can't build me a house?"

"Ouch!" he heard his uncle yelp. "Whatcha go and do that for? Same spot you hit me on just before dinner. Lawd, woman. You wanna knock all the sense outta me?"

"You ain't got no sense to knock out."

"That's 'cause you done knocked it all out yesterday."

"Wouldn't have to if you didn't give that boy those records and run off his wife."

Edward quietly hung up the phone as they continued to bicker about the value of James Brown on a marriage and headed back downstairs before calling the police in the hope that perhaps he'd missed a note somewhere. He'd hate to sound like a fool on the phone only to find out that his wife was at the supermarket.

Just as he reached the bottom, the front door opened and Denise walked in.

Relief flooded through him and he almost rushed to her and swept her up in his arms. But he didn't.

"Where have you been, Denise? I was worried sick. This isn't like you to just run off without a word," he chastised, like a parent scolding a child.

Denise walked past him without a word of acknowledgment, opened the closet door and hung up her jacket, then set her purse on the top shelf. She closed the closet door and walked into the kitchen.

For several moments Edward stood rooted to the spot with his mouth open. He shook his head and followed her.

"Did you hear what I said?" he asked, storming into the kitchen.

Denise took a teacup from the hook beneath the sink, filled it with water, and stuck it in the microwave. She pressed in the numbers, hit start, folded her arms, and waited.

"Denise, I'm talking to you," he said, growing more frustrated by the minute. What had gotten into her? *Must be those talk shows,* he concluded.

The bell chimed on the microwave and Denise removed the cup, added a teabag and some sugar, walked right by him again, and went upstairs.

Edward followed her upstairs, determined to get some answers. He didn't know what was on his wife's mind, but he damned well was going to find out. The instant he crossed the threshold of the room, Denise looked up at him from the bed and his whole world came to a grinding halt.

"Edward, I want a divorce."

Three

For a moment all Edward could do was stand there. Divorce! All those years of working with drills on the construction sites had definitely affected his hearing, because he was certain he could not have heard her right. That had to be the reason why he felt as if someone had just kicked him in the head; his hearing was going bad. He shook his head to clear it and hopefully when he looked at Denise again, she would turn back into the same dependable, loving woman he'd married. But then his mind and his vision cleared and what he saw in front of him was a woman he barely recognized, from the firm line of her usually soft, pouty mouth, to the ramrod-straight back, to the look of resoluteness in her eyes that gave him a chill. He quickly donned his king-of-the-castle cape and stepped fully into the room.

"This is not a time for games, Denise," he said in his best no-nonsense voice.

"I'm not playing," she responded calmly, reaching for the nail file from the nightstand and holding it up in front of her. She stared at the point, then at him.

Reflexively Edward took a step back, as the tiny file seemed to grow to lethal proportions in front of his eyes. He'd watched enough Lifetime Channel episodes to know that the women always seemed to have a justifiable reason why they did away with the men in their lives. *Too much television, Edward,* he inwardly scolded himself. *You are not afraid of your wife.* He cleared his throat. "Fine. You're not playing and neither am I. I asked you a simple question and you give me some ridiculous response."

Suddenly Denise sprung up from her perch on the side of the bed, the nail file pointing menacingly at her husband. "Did you say ridiculous? You think divorce is ridiculous? Well, I'm glad you do, because I don't," she said, her words coming so hot and fast they stumbled over each other on their way out. "I can't take it anymore, Edward." She began to pace in front of him.

"Take what anymore?" he asked, truly baffled.

She halted in midstep and whirled toward him, throwing her arms into the air. "Everything!"

His head snapped back, his nose missing the tip

of the deadly file by mere inches. "Everything? What in the world are you talking about?" he asked and wondered if he should wrestle her for the file. If those things were now banned from airplanes they should certainly be banned from bedrooms.

Denise planted her fists on her hips. "That's just it, Edward, it would take the rest of my life to try to explain. I've spent the past twenty-seven years living for everyone except myself. I've put my needs and wants on hold for you and the kids. What I want has never factored into anyone's thinking. Just that Mom will be there to cook, clean, and say yes to everyone. Well, the kids are grown now, Edward. They're on their own. You have a thriving business. It's been clear for quite some time that none of you really need me. I'm like an old shoe—comfortable. Not anymore. I want to be a stiletto!"

A stiletto?

"I've sat on the sidelines while everyone around me built a life. Now it's my turn and I'm taking it— without you." She tossed the file on the bed and walked toward the window, turning her back to him.

Edward breathed a sigh of relief. "Denise, you can't be serious. Divorce is not something you do on a whim."

She laughed harshly. "Typical response. What makes you believe that I haven't thought about it?"

Slowly she turned around to face him and he saw the depth of her pain swimming in her eyes. *This was real.*

"You really don't know me at all, do you? After all these years," she whispered. "Everyone has grown, except me, or so you thought. I'm not the same young, impressionable girl you met all those years ago. Somewhere along the way you let go of my hand and moved on without me. You may have been here in body, but not in spirit. Not really. This hasn't been a real marriage for years. It's been an arrangement. And now I'm making arrangements to change all of that."

Gingerly he moved toward her. He knew that if he could just touch her, hold her close to his heart and let her hear the terror that beat there, she would say it was all a mistake. That she was just upset, that her hormones had gone crazy. Something, anything but what she was telling him now.

He reached for her and she stepped away, knowing that if she inhaled his scent, felt his hands on her body, her resolve would crumble as it had so many times in the past.

Stung by her reaction, he stepped back, dropping his hands to his sides. "Denise, baby, please listen to me. I know you're upset."

"Do you really, Edward? Or are you just concerned that your dinner isn't cooked?"

"That's not fair, Denise."

"Fair hasn't been a part of the equation in our marriage for a very long time."

A sudden sense of desperation seized him. He had to try another tack, some way to reach her. "Don't you love me anymore?"

Denise's body tensed. She should have known that he would toss love into the mix. "What's love got to do with it? This is not about loving you, Edward, it's about loving me." She poked her finger at her chest.

"This isn't making sense. What can I do? What *did* I do? You don't just decide to get a divorce after twenty-seven years of marriage. We have to talk about this, Denise," he pleaded. "Haven't I been a good husband, a good father, a solid provider? Have I ever cheated on you?"

"That's just it. *You've* been this entire marriage and every now and then I get to participate." She lowered her head. "And I'm tired. I want to see what I can do for Denise before it's too late."

"Look, we just need some time to think this through. Whatever it is, we can work it out. I know we can."

She refused to look at him. "I think you should sleep in Anthony's old room tonight." She turned away. "I want to be alone."

Edward's entire body went cold. "Anthony's room?" he croaked in disbelief. "Are you telling me to get out of our bedroom?" he asked, the words coming out slowly and painfully.

"Yes," she said emphatically. "I am." She breezed by him and placed her hand on the open door—waiting.

Edward stared at this stranger who had taken his wife's place. It was surreal, like the movie *Invasion of the Body Snatchers,* he thought, completely dazed by what had transpired. He had the overwhelming urge to peek under the bed for pods.

He drew in a breath. Fine, if this is what she thought she wanted, he'd go along with it for a minute. He was pretty damned sure that after a good night's sleep without him, she'd change her mind. *What if she didn't?* He strode toward the door, with not as much pep in his step as he would have liked, but he refused to beg. "Good night, Denise," he said through his teeth.

She pursed her lips, waited for him to cross the threshold, and closed the door behind him.

Somehow, Edward found his way to his son's old bedroom. He stood in the doorway and looked at the single bed, the trophies on the shelf, and the wall plastered with his favorite sports heroes: Michael Jordan and Magic Johnson. His son hadn't used this room since he'd moved out, but Denise didn't have the heart to change it.

"I want it to be just like he left it for those times when he comes home. It's comforting to know there is somewhere you can go where things are the same—familiar. Don't you think so?" she'd asked him as they'd both stood in the doorway on the day of Anthony's departure.

He'd draped his arm around her shoulder, hearing the hitch in her voice. "He's all grown up now, Dee, and so is Christine. When they come back it will only be for holidays and short visits. They have lives of their own now. They've moved on. It's just me and you."

A tear slid down her cheek. "I know," she'd whispered. "Just us." She'd eased away from his hold and walked away.

As Edward stepped into Anthony's room he wondered now if Denise had been sad because the children were gone or because all that was left was the two of them. Was he that awful to live with? A knot filled his gut. He looked down the hallway to the closed door of his bedroom. He took two steps in that direction, but stopped. No. He wasn't going to plead. He wasn't going to ask for forgiveness for something he hadn't done. What they both needed was some sleep, some time to think. Thanksgiving was in two days. The whole family would converge on the house, filling it with love and good cheer, and Denise would see for herself what she was throwing away. He'd give her the time and space she needed. But one thing he was certain of, he was getting back in his bedroom with his wife. A sudden frightening image of his aunt and uncle flashed before his eyes. If they ever found out. . . . He didn't want to think about it. This mess had to be fixed before they arrived on Thanksgiving morning.

Reluctantly, Edward closed the door and crossed the room to the narrow bed. He pulled back the quilt and slid between the cool cotton sheets. He had to get some sleep. Tomorrow was a big day with the executives from the Davidson project—the ground-breaking ceremony. The press would be there in droves. He had to be sharp. He squeezed his eyes shut and prayed for sleep.

More than an hour later he was still wide awake, staring up at the ceiling. He turned over too quickly and almost fell out of the bed. "Damnit!" he sputtered, catching himself before he hit the floor, and wondered how on earth his six-foot, one-hundred-and-eighty-pound son had ever slept in this make-believe bed.

Truly annoyed, he pulled the covers up to his chin and tried to get comfortable. He missed the warmth of Denise next to him, the sound of her soft snore, the feel of her body nestled against his.

Tossing the covers aside, he got up. "This is ridiculous," he muttered as he pulled the door open and strode down the hallway toward *his* bedroom. He turned the knob and pushed. He frowned. The door wouldn't open. *It must be stuck,* he thought and tried again. It wouldn't budge. And then it dawned on him. She'd locked him out! She'd actually locked him out. He couldn't believe it and was so stunned he couldn't move or think. His wife had lost her natural mind. That was the only explanation.

He raised his fist, but stopped. He wouldn't reduce himself to knocking on his own bedroom door. This was his house, his bedroom, and his wife. *Then why am I standing on the outside of a locked door?*

"Denise," he whispered timidly, the humiliation so intense he could barely get her name to cross his lips. He listened for any sound and then he knew he'd just entered the Twilight Zone and that this was all some bizarre nightmare episode.

Coming from the other side of the door was a wail from the Godfather of Soul, James Brown, singing "I Feel Good."

Edward whirled away and stormed back down the hallway, slamming the door behind him. Everyone had gone completely mad!

Four

Safely inside their bedroom, Denise breathed a little easier. She'd done it!

Yet, for a split second, she'd almost caved in as she'd done so many times. She loved him so desperately. She'd grabbed the fingernail file to keep from grabbing him and to give her a reason to look away. Seeing him in pain and knowing she caused it was like slicing into her own body. The only reason she hadn't given in was because she was aware that if she did, nothing would change. She'd go back to being a housekeeper and cook instead of a wife and partner.

This was for both of them.

With a click of the stereo's remote control, the rambunctious sounds of James Brown singing "I Feel Good" increased in volume. In her off-key voice, Denise joined in, doing a little spin and slide in a good imitation of James. If she didn't think she'd injure herself, she'd try a split. *I do feel good.* She'd passed the first hurdle.

Initially she'd turned on the stereo because she'd been afraid she might cry and hadn't wanted Edward to know how much asking for the divorce, even make-believe, had torn her up inside. If he had sensed any weakness, he would have pushed her or taken her into his arms and she would have lost the will to fight.

He had always been aware of the power he had over her. Her grandmother had once said if Edward led her off a cliff, she'd happily follow. Her grandmother had been right. Every time Edward picked her up, her grandmother would stare both of them in the eye and tell them to be careful. She wasn't talking about Edward driving his old Ford Pinto.

At no other time is love so desperate and the need to express that love so intense as when you're a teenager. She'd fallen in love with Edward on their second date when she'd cried in his arms after pouring out her heart to him about her parents' impending divorce.

"Letting go is hard, but if it helps, I'm here," he'd said, his strong arms around her as they sat in his car. It had.

From then on they'd spent as much time as possible together. Her grandmother teased him about charging rent, because he was at her house so much.

His comeback was that the only reason he was there so much was for her wonderful cooking. His response never failed to cause her grandmother to blush and make Denise think how lucky she was and how much she loved him.

Loving Edward had been easy. He was fun to be with, intelligent, handsome. He shared his dreams with her, held her when she was sad, and helped her adjust and make new friends in Atlanta. To express that love she let Edward go further, let him touch her in places no other man ever had. Three months after they'd started dating he'd gone from being her best friend to her boyfriend to her lover on a beautiful summer afternoon while on a picnic.

She'd been scared. He'd been gentle and patient. "I promise, Dee, I'll love you forever."

He had kept that promise, but now he had to let her live her own life.

Denise awoke on Edward's side of the bed. Instinctively her body had sought the comfort of his. She ran her hand over the cold sheet next to her. She missed him and just hoped she'd shaken him up enough to make him realize he had to let her be a partner in their marriage, and have her say in her own life. Last night had probably been as difficult for him as it had been for her.

A wicked smile curved her lips as she envisioned ways of making it up to him. She just hoped it didn't take him too long to come to his senses.

Yesterday she'd broken the tradition of being at home when he arrived to prove a point: a change had come. Time for round two.

Finally opening her eyes, she stared at the digital dial of the clock radio: 7:03 A.M. *I overslept and it feels wonderful.* Her internal clock usually went off around 6:30. Edward's alarm clock went off at 6:40. A heavy sleeper, he often ignored the alarm and she had to wake him up. A dreamy smile lit her face as she remembered that on many of those occasions he'd draw her into his arms and make love to her. Sighing with regret that she wasn't getting any of that good loving today, she rolled out of bed and headed for the shower.

Taking off her nightgown, she dropped it into the dirty clothes hamper, trying not to think of just a few days ago when Edward had joined her in the glass enclosure and they'd steamed up the shower with their own heat. It was futile.

His large, calloused hands had roamed freely over her body, building the passion and the need. That man of hers knew just where to touch her. She hadn't cared one bit that her shower cap had come off and her chemically processed hair was getting wet. Her cries of fulfillment had filled the enclosure.

Afterward, when their breathing had almost returned to normal, he'd grinned at her and said it was nice not having to worry about the kids hearing them.

Resolutely, Denise turned and went to the sunken tub across the room. She could fight herself, Edward, and memories, but not all three at the same time.

Fifteen minutes later, Denise walked into the kitchen expecting Edward to be making his usual mess. A couple of years ago she'd had the flu and he'd been completely inept. She'd wanted to cry when she'd come downstairs after he'd left for work and seen the wreck he'd made of her beautiful kitchen. He'd been so pleased with the hard scrambled eggs and overcooked pan sausage he'd brought on a tray. At least the toast hadn't been burned. He could be the most thoughtful man in the world, or the most stubborn.

Her brows bunched when she didn't see him. He was probably getting dressed for his big meeting today. Continuing across the room, she went to the refrigerator and began pulling out sausage and eggs. She was hungry. Edward, as she had told him, was on his own.

In a short time breakfast was ready and still Edward hadn't arrived. Denise frowned. It wasn't likely he'd left without talking to her. She'd heard him try the locked door last night. That had to have made him angry. He'd gone back to Anthony's room, as she'd suspected he would, but he'd be back. He was relentless when he wanted something. And he wanted his life back the way it was.

Picking up a plate, Denise filled it with grits, soft scrambled eggs, perfect sausage patties, and light, fluffy biscuits, then took a seat at the end of the island. He'd soon learn that it was no longer what he wanted, but what *she* intended to get.

Five

Edward was jerked awake when his two-hundred-pound body hit the floor. He groaned and rubbed his hip, then his shoulder. "What the . . . ?" He looked around through half-opened lids. It took him a couple of minutes to orient himself as the room slowly came into focus and then the night before. His pulse picked up a beat. *Denise locked me out. I spent the night in my son's bedroom. I am forty-seven years old and I just fell out of bed.* If it wasn't so horrible it could almost be funny.

He held his watch up to his face and squinted. 8:45 A.M. He struggled to his feet, using the side of the bed for leverage. Then it hit him: 8:45! His meeting started in just over an hour, followed by the ground-breaking. Was Denise that upset with him that she wouldn't even wake him up? She woke him every morning. He depended on her. She knew how hard he slept. At least he pretended to sleep hard. He liked to watch her from the corner of his eyes as she moved around the bedroom in the morning and then tiptoe over to whisper in his ear, "Time to wake up, baby." Ooh, how he loved that. Her warm breath right up against his ear would raise his testosterone level to mammoth heights. Just thinking about her made his juices rise. He looked down at the tent in his shorts and thought about all the ways Denise made it go away. Then reality bit him. *Denise wants a divorce.*

Edward darted out of the bedroom and half limped, half sprinted down the hallway, determined that if the door was locked he was breaking it down with his good hip and shoulder.

He turned the knob and the door sprung open. His gaze zeroed in on the bed, which was neatly made and empty. Where was Denise? The clock on the nightstand read 8:50. As much as he wanted to deal with the crisis at hand, he would certainly have a mega one brewing if this Davidson project fell apart. He had a staff and their families that he was responsible for. He wouldn't let them down. This craziness between him and Denise would be settled tonight once and for all. And then maybe life could get back to normal.

Showered, shaved, and decked out in the new suit Denise had insisted that he purchase, Edward adjusted his tie in the mirror and had to admit that the midnight blue Armani suit fit as if it was made for him. He remembered the conversation he and Denise had about his wardrobe. "If you are going to be successful, then look the part," she'd admonished as she dragged him through the men's department of Saks. "You can't go on television or turn up on the front page of the *Atlanta Journal* with jeans and chambray shirts all the time. You've come a long way from the storefront, honey."

He *had* come a long way, he admitted as he dabbed on some cologne and clipped his cell phone to the waistband of his pants. As a businessman his abilities were unquestionable, and until last night he would have thought the same of himself as a husband.

Taking a deep breath, he pulled away from his reflection and headed downstairs, hoping to at least grab a cup of coffee before he hit the road. Hopefully, Denise would have been kind enough to put a pot on, even though the aroma of freshly brewed coffee was not in the air.

She heard him grumbling before she saw him. Even impeccably dressed, he looked as miserable as she felt.

When he entered the kitchen he was surprised to find Denise sitting at the kitchen table, sipping a cup of tea with a plate of half-eaten food in front of her. If he didn't know better, he'd swear she looked totally rested and relaxed as if last night hadn't happened.

"Good morning," he murmured, testing the waters.

She barely looked up. "'Morning," she said and snapped open the newspaper.

"Uh, the big groundbreaking is this morning. I should have been at the office already," he said, hoping that normalcy had returned.

"Oh . . . is that today? I forgot." She sighed, took a sip of her tea, and continued reading the paper. "Good luck," she added over the top of the page, barely looking up. "I'm sure it will be fine." She turned toward the window. "Radio said we're expecting a major storm today. Hurricane watch. Don't forget your umbrella." She went back to reading.

He swallowed, suddenly unsure of how to talk to her, how to reach this woman he'd loved and lived with most of his life. His heart ached with a kind of emptiness that he couldn't explain. He wanted to tell her how scared he was, but he didn't know how and wasn't sure if she would listen. But he had to try.

"Denise . . . about last night . . . you really didn't mean what you said. Did you? You were just upset. If you would only tell me what's wrong, I'll fix it."

"It's too late to fix it, Edward. And sometimes, whether you believe it or not, *you* can't fix everything. That's part of the problem. Our marriage is not one of your construction projects. I've thought about it, thought about us. It's not working and hasn't for a very long time. You and the kids have your life and I want to have mine."

"Why are you so dead set into believing that we can't have the life you want together? Is divorce the only answer?" he asked, his frustration mounting.

"It's the only answer for me. Do you really think I'm taking all of this lightly? I'm not. This marriage has been all about you, what you want, how you want it. I can't even have a conversation with the kids without them making sure it's okay with you first. What kind of marriage is that? What kind of relationship is that to have with your children? I don't want this to turn into something ugly, Edward. I won't wind up like my parents—at each other's throats, bickering and fighting, unwilling to let go."

"I can't let you do this," he said, instinctively returning to the self he knew best—take charge.

She laughed harshly. "Do you hear yourself?" She shook her head. "I'm sure you don't. You never have." She took a sip of her tea, then absently stirred the grits with her fork. "You'll miss your big event if you don't hurry," she added, her voice devoid of emotion.

He glanced at the clock, then at his wife, torn between his responsibilities. For the first time in his life he felt totally incapable, inept, and unable to put the pieces together. The realization left him confused and reeling.

"Take your umbrella," she reminded him again.

"We're going to talk this out when I get home tonight, Denise. I don't want another night like last night. No matter what you might think or believe, I missed you."

Denise finally turned to look at him and for a split second he saw the same misery swimming in her eyes that was in his. His hopes rose. Maybe, just maybe, she was feeling as bad about this as he was.

She pressed her lips together, took a deep breath, and looked him straight in the eye. "I want to sell the house." With that, she rose from her seat and walked out, leaving him with his mouth open.

For several moments he stood there in stunned silence, until finally he heard the door to their bedroom slam shut. He blinked and somehow found his way to the front door and outside to his SUV. His eyes burned and his stomach rolled dangerously. It was all he could do to stick the key in the ignition.

Behind the wheel of his Escalade, Edward could barely keep his attention focused on the road. His thoughts jumped around like jackrabbits in a meadow. One minute he was thinking about the unbelievable twist in what he thought was his stable marriage, the next he was thinking about what to say in front of the camera, then his thoughts would swing back to the look in Denise's eyes and the emptiness in her voice. And her final statement—"I want to sell the house." *The house that I built for them.* He was so stunned he still couldn't respond. His whole life was coming apart at the seams and he had no idea how to put it back together.

The clock on the dash read 9:40. His meeting started in twenty minutes and he still had at least another forty before he would arrive at his office. He slammed his palm against the steering wheel. His well-ordered life was falling apart. What was happening?

Six

Edward found his way to work by pure instinct. By the time he arrived, the meeting was already in session in the company's conference room. William Henry, sitting at the head of the table, jumped up and met Edward at the door.

"Hey, man, everything okay? We were getting worried and the suits from Davidson were getting pissed. The press is here too, chomping at the bit. But I held everyone off with my incredible charm." He chuckled.

Edward tried to focus, put his mind on the task at hand and not the drama that was happening in his household. He'd always prided himself on being able to separate business from his home life, but today he didn't know if he had what it took to get through the rest of the day.

"Yeah, fine. Sorry I'm late. Car wouldn't start," he offered up as an excuse.

William patted him on the back. "Well, now that

you're here, let's get this party started. Did you have to get it towed or just a boost?"

Edward looked at him curiously. "What?"

"The car. Did you get it started or did it need to be towed?"

"Oh. Uh, hey, I got a boost," he lied.

"You sure you're okay? You look like you haven't slept."

The previous night ran through his head like a bad movie. "I'm cool. Let's do this. I don't want to keep them waiting any longer than I already have."

After making his apologies, the balance of the meeting went smoothly. The heads of the Davidson group were pleased with the proposal and signed off on all the documents to the flash of the news media's cameras. They all posed for the standard grin-and-grip shot, then piled into cars for the official groundbreaking ceremony on the other side of town.

By the time the groups arrived at the site, the skies had turned a dangerous gray. Rolls of thunder could be heard in the background even as the legion of speakers took their turns at the microphone.

The mayor of Atlanta stepped up to the mic and they all instinctively knew that with it being an election year, whatever the good mayor had to say was going to be long.

"I'm honored to stand before you today on such a momentous occasion for the citizens of Atlanta . . ."

William leaned over and whispered to Edward, "The sky is going to open up any minute, and I don't think this tent is going to do us much good."

"Hmmm," Edward murmured, just willing the day to be over so that he could get back home. He needed to speak to his wife. Their life together was coming apart and he was clueless as to the reason why. It seemed that overnight his wife had turned into someone that he no longer knew; an unhappy woman, who, according to the little Denise divulged, had been unhappy for a long time. How could he not have known? Had he been so involved in his own life, building a life for them, that he'd missed all the cues?

"Look, I don't want to get in your business, but is everything okay at home?" William asked, cutting into Edward's thoughts. "I know we have things locked down here. But I've never seen you so distracted, especially with something this major going on."

Edward turned to his friend of more than ten years. William had been there with him from the early days of his storefront. He'd helped him build the business from the ground up. Edward had been the best man at William's wedding and they'd spent many a weekend sharing a beer over a sports game.

There was a part of him that desperately needed to bare his soul, to share his angst, fear, and confusion. Yet there was that other part, that "gotta be a man" part, that dictated he keep his own counsel, fight his own battles. And that realization made him feel so very alone.

"Everything is fine at home. You know, the usual stuff, getting ready for the holidays, bills, the kids."

"Kids okay?"

"Yes." At least that much was true. "Christine and Reese are settling into his work routine and Anthony seems to be hot and heavy with his new girlfriend. She's supposed to drop by for Thanksgiving after she visits her folks."

William chuckled. "Anthony? Serious about a girl? Who would have thought it?"

Edward smiled, thinking of his son and how he'd matured over the past two years. He had a good job, decent apartment, was a respectful young man, and now might be on the brink of settling down. He was proud of Anthony. They'd done a good job raising him and his sister. *They.* It had taken two of them to raise the children. Two of them to build a life, a family, security. How could Denise ever believe that she was not part of the process?

The drone of the mayor's speech filtered into Edward's thoughts. He checked his watch. There were at least two more hours of this back-patting to go and then he could head home. But suddenly, as if someone had hit a switch, all the power went out; the microphones sputtered and died and the huge lighting lamps flashed and went dark. The sky turned pitch black and the heavens opened up in a torrent of blinding rain. Everyone outside of the tent ran for cover, followed by those beneath, as a mighty gust of wind ripped the tent from its stakes, sending it flying across the field.

"Run for the car, man!" William called out over the roar of wind and rain.

"Right behind you."

Edward ran against the wind, trying to get to his car, when one of the speakers that was perched on a platform was thrown through the air, knocking William to the ground. Edward darted around fallen debris to his friend's side.

"Will, Will . . ."

William groaned and slowly pulled himself to his knees.

Rain and wind whipped around them, making it impossible to see.

"Can you get up?"

"I think so."

"Let me help you." He put his arm around William and pulled him to his feet. With all the strength he could summon he half walked, half dragged William to his SUV.

Barely able to see out of the window, Edward could still make out the devastation. He shook his head in disbelief. Denise mentioned rain, but no umbrella made by man could have helped today.

"Bad storm," William murmured.

"Let me see if I can get the news." He reached toward the dial on the radio and after long moments of static he was finally able to locate a news station. And the news was not good. Roads were washed out and flash flood conditions were in effect across the state, with dangerous lightning and power outages. Hurricane warnings were in effect throughout the night.

"Oh, man," Edward said. "I've got to get home."

"There's no way we can make that trip," William said, rubbing the knot on the back of his head. "Maybe we can make it to the office and hole up there."

Edward peered out of the window and was able to make out the headlights of the vehicles as they slowly eased their way out of the field.

"You're right. We can't stay here. It's too dangerous. I need to call home and make sure Denise is okay." He reached for his cell phone, but it was gone. He slapped his hand against the dashboard. "You have your cell with you?"

"It's in my car back at the office. I left it in the charger."

"How's your head?" Edward asked as he put the car in gear.

"Feels like I've been hit in the head with a speaker." He tried to laugh, but groaned instead.

"As soon as we get back to the office we'll get some ice on that knot."

What should have been a twenty-minute drive turned into a two-hour marathon of slow going through blinding rain, dodging downed trees and power lines and being rerouted through flooded areas. Finally they pulled into the parking lot and made it into the building.

Edward's secretary Lena jumped up from her desk the moment they entered.

"Mr. Morrison, Mr. Henry, thank goodness. We were all so worried." Then she took a look at William and her hand flew to her mouth in alarm. "Oh, no, Mr. Henry, you've been hurt. Let me get you some ice." She darted off before they could say a word.

"I'm going to my office and stretch out on the couch," William said, holding a handkerchief to his forehead.

"I'll check on you in a few," Edward said, just as the lights blinked off and then on again. "The generator must have kicked on. I better try to call Denise."

He went to Lena's desk and called home. The

phone barely rang once before it was picked up by Christine.

"Christine?"

"Dad. We were worried. Are you okay?"

"Yes. I'm fine, sweetheart. What are you doing there? Is your mother all right?"

"She's fine. I took today off and when I heard the weather report I decided to come over today. Anthony and Aunt Etta and Uncle Eddie are here too. I guess they thought the same thing. No one wanted to miss Mom's Thanksgiving dinner."

"Is your mom around?"

"I'll get her. How long do you think you'll be?"

"I don't know, sweetheart. All the roads are either closed or flooded. And it doesn't look like the rain is going to let up."

"Oh no," she moaned. "Let me get Mom."

Edward waited with his heart in his throat. He had no idea what kind of reception he would receive from Denise.

"Hello. Ed?"

"Hi. I just wanted to make sure you were all right."

"I'm okay. The kids are here and your aunt and uncle. Will you be able to make it home?"

"I don't know. It looks like I might have to wait it out. But the minute they give the all-clear, I'll head home."

A long moment of silence hung between them.

"Guess I should have taken my umbrella, huh?" He tried to laugh.

"You just be careful, Ed," she said softly. "Call if you can't make it tonight."

"I will," he said, matching her tone, and hoping that the concern he heard in her voice was real and not his imagination. "Denise . . . about last night, and this morning . . ."

She lowered her voice. "I don't think this is a good time to talk, Ed."

He swallowed. "I guess you're right. But we have to. I need you to help me understand why you don't want to be married to me anymore."

"Mom!" Christine called out in the background. "Aunt Etta is in the pots," she singsonged.

"We'll talk, Ed. But I'd better go before Etta adds some of her 'special' ingredients to my gravy."

"Sure. I'll call later."

"'Bye."

Slowly he hung up the phone and wondered for the hundredth time how he was going to fix what was wrong with his marriage.

Seven

Edward found it hard to imagine that any night could have been more difficult than the one before, but this night took the cake. Not only was he not in bed with his wife or at the very least banished to his son's old bedroom, he was knotted up on a love seat in his office, stuck until morning. Instead of the gentle soft snore of his wife, he was rocked and rolled by the inhumane rumbling of William, who'd decided to camp out on the leather recliner.

"I'm gonna stay in here with you, man," William had announced, once it was determined that travel for the night was out of the question. "I heard that if you had a head injury you needed to be monitored in case you slip into a coma. You got my back, right?"

"Sure. I'll keep an ear out for you. But I'm pretty sure you're fine. I've seen enough episodes of *ER* where the patients had head injuries. There've been no signs of dizziness or nausea," he said with authority.

"You sure know your stuff," William said, as he made himself comfortable in the chair.

But now, hours later, eyeing William from bleary, sleep-deprived eyes, as much as Edward cared about him, he would pay big money to *put* him in a coma, anything to shut up the herd of buffalos that William expelled every time he breathed. Morning couldn't get there fast enough. He would rather stay mystified by his wife's totally bizarre behavior than to spend another night in the same room with William Henry. The only conclusion he could come to was that he was paying for some misdeed in a prior life. He closed his eyes and prayed for deliverance.

The light tap on his office door stirred him from a fitful sleep. Slowly he opened his eyes. He looked around. It was the same nightmare. He groaned as he tried to unravel his body and sit up. On stiff legs and with an aching back, he made his way to the door.

"'Morning, Mr. Morrison," Lena murmured. "The news report says that the roads are open. Thought you'd want to know."

"Thanks, Lena." He rubbed his eyes and yawned.

Lena peered around him. "What's that noise?" she asked, looking very concerned.

Edward looked over his shoulder and twisted his mouth into a grimace. "The creature from the black lagoon," he said and meant it.

Lena giggled. "Anyway . . . I'm going to head home. The staff that were stuck here are heading out as well."

He rotated his neck. "Drive safely."

"You too, sir. And happy Thanksgiving. Give my best to your family."

"I will. You do the same."

"Enjoy your day." She turned and left.

Enjoy my day. He had no idea what awaited him at home, but whatever it was he would be prepared. At least he hoped so.

By the time he arrived at home, tired, gritty, and in desperate need of a hot shower, Thanksgiving at the Morrison household was in full swing. He could hear music and laughter the moment he entered the door, with Uncle Eddie having everyone in stitches doing his version of the James Brown slide.

When Edward walked into the living room, Uncle Eddie had donned an old blanket and thrown it over his shoulders as a cape. He was hunched over, singing "Please, Please, Please." Anthony played the famous sidekick Maceo by replacing the cape each time Eddie threw it off in the throes of his performance.

Edward couldn't help but laugh at the scene and he had to admit that the old man was pretty good, right down to the pressed, shoulder-length hair and platform shoes. Aunt Etta was beaming like a schoolgirl as she sipped what he knew was not iced tea, unless iced tea was being refilled from the flask in her purse. And even Denise had a smile on her face and the old sparkle was back in her eyes. If he didn't know better, he'd bet money that all was as it should be. But he knew better.

"Happy Thanksgiving, everybody!" he greeted, stepping into the room.

All eyes turned in his direction. Christine was the first one at his side and in his arms.

"Dad," she greeted effusively, giving him a big kiss on the cheek. "Uncle Eddie was keeping us entertained until dinner."

"So I see," he said with a chuckle. "How are you, baby girl, and where is that son-in-law of mine?"

Christine's expression darkened. "Working. He tried to get out of it," she offered in his defense. "But the new residents always have to pull the holiday and graveyard shifts."

"Hang in there, baby girl." He gently patted her

back and looked at Denise. "It will all work out. Don't you think so, Dee?"

"Reese is a good man. I'm sure he and Christine will get through this rough time," Denise offered, deftly sidestepping Edward's real question.

"Hey, Dad," Anthony said, stepping up to his father and giving him the one-fisted hug. "You look a little worse for wear."

"Thanks, son, always the bearer of good cheer." Edward chuckled. "Is your lady friend going to be able to join us?"

Anthony shrugged. "I hope so. I may have to go and pick her up. Depends on when her folks finish up dinner. I really do want you all to meet her. She's hot!" He rubbed his hands together.

"Anthony!" Denise mildly reprimanded. "Is that how you describe your girlfriend?"

Anthony chuckled. "Absolutely!"

"Thatta boy," Uncle Eddie said. "As long as they stays hot you can have fun putting out the fire! Ain't that right, Etta?"

"You old fool." She popped him in the head with a pillow. "Sit down and stop filling that boy's head with your foolishness."

"Foolishness! You didn't say that last night." He howled with laughter.

Anthony looked from his great-uncle to his great-aunt. "How old are you two anyway?" he asked, totally unable to believe that they could possibly have any spark left in the tank.

"Old enough to teach you a thing or two, boy. Ask your daddy, taught that boy everything he knows. Ask your mama. She'll verify it. Ain't that right, Dee?"

Denise put her hand over her mouth to keep from bursting out laughing. "I think it's time for dinner. Let's adjourn to the dining room," she replied instead.

The troupe happily filed into the dining room, animatedly discussing the validity of Uncle Eddie's claims, leaving Denise and Edward alone.

She turned to Edward. "Why don't you go shower and change while I get the food out on the table?"

"Can't I even get a hello?" he whispered. "Didn't you miss me just a little bit?"

Denise opened her mouth to speak, just as Etta's voice rose from the kitchen in concert with the banging sounds of pots.

"I know what I'm doing! If you need to heat up the food, put the gas on high! Pass me the hot sauce."

"You better go tend to *your* aunt," Edward murmured, knowing how Denise maintained complete domain over the kitchen.

"*My* aunt! That's *your* bloodline. We're only related by marriage," she tossed over her shoulder as she hurried into the kitchen, panic etched on her face.

"But for how long?" he whispered as he headed upstairs to shower and change.

Eight

Your father and I have decided to get a divorce," Denise announced and watched shock spread around the table. For the first time Aunt Etta actually appeared at a loss for words. Uncle Eddie looked at his nephew as if expecting him to say it was all a joke.

Denise hadn't planned on making the announcement at dinner, but after seeing Edward's desolate expression when he returned and worrying half the night that he was injured, she'd been afraid of weakening. Even now, she had to clench her hands to keep from walking over and touching him to reassure herself that he was unharmed. But it was the shocked faces of her children that wrenched Denise's heart and almost caused her to forget the whole idea.

Anthony simply stared as her as if he couldn't get

his mind to reconcile with what she'd just said. Christine had no such difficulty. She was as volatile in her reaction as Denise had expected.

"No! You can't!" Her frantic gaze snapped from one parent to the other, finally resting on her father, the person she had always gone to when she was hurt or in need of advice or just a hug. "Daddy?"

Edward, who had glanced down at his barely touched plate of food when Denise had begun talking, raised his head, but instead of looking at his daughter he looked at her. Denise clenched her hands so tightly her nails dug into her palms. She refused to be swayed by the pain in his tired, bleary eyes. She simply couldn't go on as they had before. He had succeeded in his business while she was not even allowed to try.

She deeply regretted she wasn't able to confide in her children, but knowing how much they loved their father, she hadn't been sure they wouldn't have told him the whole thing was a hoax. Reese's absence also created a problem. She had counted on him being there with Christine.

Finally, Edward's gaze swung to Christine's and for the first time Denise wondered if he would paint her in a bad light to her children. He could, if he wanted. They had always loved him the best.

"Your mother and I are having some problems,"

he said, as if each word were being ripped from his heart.

"You work through problems," Anthony blurted, his boyishly handsome face pinched with concern. "You don't get a divorce."

"He's right, Eddie," Aunt Etta said, jabbing her fork in the direction of her nephew. "You got the children and too much invested in this house and each other."

"We're selling the house," Denise said calmly, although her nerves were jumpy. Edward had to believe this was real. She was determined to find out exactly how much she and their marriage meant to him.

"What?" Christine came to her feet. "Daddy built this house! We grew up here."

Denise expected the outburst and her daughter's first thoughts to be of her father. "It's settled. The house is too big for either of us to maintain on our own."

"Daddy?" Christine said. Her voice sounded frightened, the way it had when she was scared of monsters in the dark and her father had to go in her room to scare them away.

Denise's hand felt numb she held them so tightly. She was sorry she had to put her children through this, but she couldn't back down now.

"We discussed selling the house," he repeated dully.

"I've already contacted a realtor," Denise said calmly, picking up her glass of iced tea.

The flatness in Edward's dark brown eyes vanished. They blazed as he leaned forward in his seat. "You called them already?"

She wouldn't shrink from his anger or feel bad that she had finally taken a step without his permission. "I saw no reason to wait."

"Just like you saw no reason to at least wait until dinner was finished," he accused, with just enough bite in his tone to raise Denise's own temper.

"Dinner *was* finished. All that was left was clearing the table and since I'm always left to do that alone, as well as wash all the dishes by myself, I decided to tell them now," she shot back.

Edward started, then he said, "We help."

Denise tsked. She was not even going to dignify that out-and-out lie with a reply. They ran from the kitchen like a stampeding herd of wildebeest being chased by a lion to watch football on the TV.

"What about Christmas when we all get together?" Anthony almost whined.

Looking in her son's lost eyes, the pressure in Denise's chest increased and she almost gave in, but she stiffened her back once again. Perhaps he needed a wake-up call as well. She still did his laundry and picked up his dry cleaning. "I'm not sure where I'll be, but you're welcome to come over."

"But it won't be the same," Anthony said, looking at his father. "So that's why there weren't any lights on the house or on the lawn?"

"I just didn't see the point," Edward said, his attention on Denise again. The gazes of the children followed.

Christine was the first to say what was on everyone's mind. "Who asked for the divorce?"

Denise and Edward stared across the end of the table at each other.

"Daddy works like a dog to give Mama everything she wants," Anthony said.

"Mama, you've always been there for us," Christine said.

"He treats her like a queen," Aunt Etta said.

Uncle Eddie nodded in agreement with his wife. "The boy never even looked at another woman. Don't know why he should 'cause she treats him like a king."

"Mama, Daddy, what were you thinking?" Christine cried. "You can't sell the only home Anthony and I remember. You're ruining the holidays for all of us!"

Denise stared at the accusing faces and rose regally to her feet. "I've spent the past twenty-seven years giving to everyone except myself. For the most part, none of you have ever noticed me unless it was time for dinner or you needed something

sewn. You wouldn't be upset now if this weren't in-
terfering with your plans for the holidays. Well, I
suggest you make other arrangements." She tossed
her napkin on the table. "This queen is abdicating
her throne."

Denise's righteous anger carried her to the attic,
where she flung herself into a chair. Pressing her
arm across her eyes, she wondered if she might have
gone a bit too far and how long she could keep up
the charade.

Nine

Edward went through his dresser drawer and shoved his necessities into an overnight bag. He went to the closet and pulled out his pressed shirts, a sports jacket, two pairs of slacks, and two ties. He took his shaving kit from the bathroom and dumped that in the bag as well. He had enough supplies to last at least two days. Enough time for Denise to come to her senses and beg for him to come back. *Let's just see how long she manages without me.* Two could play at this crazy game, he concluded. As much as he dreaded spending a minute more than necessary with his aunt and uncle, he took them up on their offer to stay with them.

After Denise's pronouncement at the dinner table, Uncle Eddie had pulled him to the side and whispered his version of sage advice.

"You know how women have those spells," he

said, looking around to be sure Etta was out of earshot.

"Spells?" Edward asked, perplexed.

"Yeah, you know what I mean, boy. PBS."

Edward tried not to laugh. "You mean PMS, Uncle Eddie?"

"Whatever. That thing that makes 'em crazy. Well, I done discovered the cure."

"Really?" He tried to contain his humor. "And what might that be, Uncle Eddie?"

"Head for the hills, boy, until they come back to themselves. When you come home, they'll be just as loving as a newborn baby. Works like a charm." He lowered his voice and looked around again. "And believe me, I know all about those spells. You come stay with me and Etta till Denise's spell passes."

"You and Aunt Etta?" he said, alarm raising his voice. Nothing could be that bad. But the truth was, maybe Uncle Eddie was right in a way. A few nights out of the house may be just the thing Denise needed to snap her out of her insanity. All he'd have to do was sleep there. He wouldn't have to deal with them for any length of time. Besides, he was confident he'd be back home in a heartbeat.

"All right. But just for a night or two," he finally agreed.

"Thatta boy." Uncle Eddie slapped him on the back. "What you really need is a man-to-man talk.

And I'm just the one to give it to you. Grab some things. We'll be outside." Uncle Eddie ambled off to the beck and call of his wife.

"Man-to-man talk," he groaned. Just what he needed. *What have I agreed to?* he thought, as he zipped his bag and headed downstairs.

His daughter and son were at the bottom of the landing, looking up at him as he came down the stairs.

"Oh, Daddy," Christine said sadly, wrapping her arms around him. She pressed her head against his chest. "You're not really going to stay with Aunt Etta and Uncle Eddie, are you?" she whispered. "You know they drive you crazy."

"It will be fine," he assured her, and kissed the top of her head. "Call me if you need anything. Me and Mom will work this out. We just need some time away from each other."

She stepped back and looked into his eyes. "But Aunt Etta and Uncle Eddie?"

Edward's stomach knotted at the prospect, but it was too late to back out now. He certainly wasn't going to move in with the newlyweds, and Anthony's lifestyle was a little too risqué for him. The less he knew the better. And another night on the love seat in his office was out of the question. "They go to bed early and I get home late," he finally said.

"Does this mean I come from a broken home?" Anthony asked, half in jest.

"You're a little old to come from a broken home, silly," Christine admonished. "Can't you be serious for one minute?"

"I'm sorry, O great big sister. But I just find it too hard to believe." He slung his hands in his pockets.

"Well, believe it. You heard Mom."

"Okay, cut it out. You both sound like two little bickering kids," Edward warned. "We don't need you two at each other's throats too."

"Sorry," they murmured in unison.

"I'm going to go home with Eddie and Etta. You two are going home. Your mother and I will work it out."

"Do you really think so, Dad?" Christine asked.

"Of course. Haven't I always been able to fix things around here? Have I ever let you or your brother down?"

Christine and Anthony shook their heads.

"All right then. Go on home, get some rest, and before you know it everything will be back to normal." He hugged his daughter and son, took one last look around his home, then headed out to the waiting car.

The last time he'd lived under the same roof with his aunt and uncle he'd been nineteen years old. Unfortunately, nothing had changed. The instant he crossed their threshold, he was no longer a forty-seven-year-old man with a wife, kids, house, and a thriving business, but a teenage boy who was instructed on what to do, from making sure he brushed his teeth to being informed that he was not to bring any of his friends home without one of them being there.

He looked around at the small but neatly furnished room. At least it had a full-size bed, he thought, consoling himself. He sat on the side and wondered how things could have gotten so bad. He was still in shock that Denise would make that kind of announcement at the dinner table. This was serious. And serious situations required serious measures. He would approach this the same way he approached a new project: lay out all of the possibilities and take the best course of action.

"It's after nine o'clock, Edward," his aunt called out from the other side of the door. "Time for bed. You need your rest."

Edward lowered his head, shook it, and groaned. "Yes, Aunt Etta."

"All right, now. Don't make me have to come in there."

He heard her shuffle down the hall in the same ratty slippers she'd worn when he was sixteen.

Some things never change, he mused, a wry grin curving his mouth.

He was just about to take off his shoes when there was a stealthy tap on the door.

"Yes?"

"Sssshhh," Uncle Eddie whispered before tiptoeing inside. "I just wanted to tell you . . . don't pay attention to any noise you might hear during the night."

"Noise?"

"Yeah, you know . . ." he said with a wink.

Edward's eyebrows rose in understanding. "Sure, Uncle Eddie. Don't worry about me."

Eddie patted him on the back. "See you in the morning." He tiptoed back out, closing the door quietly behind him.

Edward undressed and slid beneath the covers. As soon as he'd closed his eyes, he heard the distinct sounds of his aunt and uncle's bed doing the two-step. He put the pillow over his head to drown out his aunt's wails of ecstasy. How old were they anyway? No wonder his aunt wanted him to go to sleep early. It was an old trick he and Denise used on their own kids.

He missed her. Desperately. And he would do whatever was necessary to get their marriage back on track. If only he could figure out where they'd gone so wrong.

"Oh, *James!*" Etta cried.

Edward burrowed farther down beneath the blanket. Maybe there was something to this James Brown thing.

Ten

Christine bit her lip to keep from crying as she rode the elevator to the third floor of Community Hospital. The shiny red garland strung around a glass-enclosed bulletin board made her think all the more how this Christmas holiday was going to be the worst ever. She had to see Reese. She had never felt so helpless or so lost as she had on seeing her father drive off behind Aunt Etta and Uncle Eddie. He loved his father's youngest brother and his wife, but they drove him crazy.

Christine sniffed. Her father had looked so pitiful coming down the stairs with his bag. He didn't say so, but Christine had seen him come out of Anthony's old room before dinner. Her mother had put him out of her bed, *and* her life. How could she have done that to a wonderful man like her father? Her mother has always been so dependable . . . so quiet. What had happened to make them want to end what

Christine thought was a perfect marriage and disrupt all of their lives? Including hers.

The elevator door slid open on the medical-surgical floor and Christine stepped out, then went directly to the nurses' station. More red garland mixed with green hung from the waist-high partition. Several silver cardboard snowflakes hung from the ceiling. Everyone was gearing up for the holidays. She had been too . . . until her mother's announcement. It was almost 9:00, visiting hours were over, and the hospital eerily quiet. "I'm Mrs. Evans, Dr. Reese Evans's wife. Is he on the floor?"

The eyes of a woman in surgical scrubs whose name tag identified her as a registered nurse widened for a fraction, then she glanced uneasily behind her to another woman dressed the same way. The other woman smirked, then said, "He's in the lounge two doors down."

"Thank you," Christine said and left, dismissing the strange attitude of the women until she pushed open the door to the lounge and saw her husband standing very close to a woman. Reese's back was to her and he didn't see Christine. The woman saw her, smiled, then slid her arms around his neck, pressing her body to his in one practiced move.

"Reese!" Christine shrieked. Shock and anger locked her in her tracks.

Reese sprang back, pulling the clinging woman's

arms from around his neck. He blinked behind his wire-rimmed glasses.

"Honey." Reese gulped, then stepped away from the other woman. "It's not what you think. I was just trying to help Loretta feel better after Swanson jumped all over her for nothing." Frowning, he threw a confused glance at the silent woman beside him. "I don't know how it happened."

Christine did. She recognized Loretta immediately. This wasn't the first time she had seen the brazen woman in her husband's face. The smug expression the woman wore said it wouldn't be the last. Christine took a deep, calming breath. Snatching her weave out by the roots might be satisfying, but it was more important to speak with Reese. He had always been able to ground her, to steady her. Outside of her father, he was the most honest, dependable man she knew. Which was probably another reason hair wasn't scattered all over the lounge.

"Reese, I need to talk with you."

"Sure, honey," he said and started toward her.

"Wait," Loretta said with a girlish giggle. "You can't go anyplace with my lipstick on your shirt collar." Planting herself in front of him, she ineffectually brushed at the red smear on the white collar Christine had ironed that morning.

Christine spun on her heel. If she stayed one more second—

"Christine," Reese called, catching up with her outside the lounge and swinging her around. "I swear it didn't mean anything!"

Christine stared at her husband and wondered how any man who had always been in the top one percent of his class since grade school could be so dense. "That woman is after you."

He blinked, then smiled boyishly at her. It was the same smile that always went straight to her heart; because he was usually so serious, the smiles were so precious. He leaned over to kiss her and Christine pulled back. "Honey, she's just an old friend. You got this all wrong."

Before Christine could speak, the door behind them opened and Loretta came out. Christine considered sticking her foot out to trip the wanton nurse, then dismissed the idea because Reese would rush to her aid and once again he'd have his hands on her . . . exactly where the hussy wanted them. "She wants more than friendship. She hugged you after she saw me. She wanted to make trouble."

Reese had the audacity to smile. "Loretta isn't that type of woman. We've known each other since my first year in med school. I was trying to comfort her and must have finally gotten her to see that she's a wonderful staff nurse when you walked in." He shrugged. "In any case, it's over and it doesn't matter."

Christine felt steam rise through the top of her head. "It doesn't matter, huh?" She glanced around and saw a surgical resident on Reese's rotation. "What if I went over there and sought a little comfort from Dr. Blair?"

"That's not funny," Reese said, his hands tightening on her arms.

Christine was too hot to take comfort in his jealousy. "It wasn't meant to be. If you want me to believe you, then don't let yourself be caught in that woman's clutches again."

Reese's dark eyebrows lifted. "She's one of the best nurses on this floor. I depend on her for my patients' care. You're getting all worked up over nothing."

Christine barely kept from sputtering, she was so incensed. "Perhaps because my life is in turmoil, perhaps I need a little comfort, but first I have to push another woman out of the way," she said, her voice trembling.

His concern was immediate. "Honey, what's the matter?" he asked, bending down to stare into her face.

"Would you care?" Christine sniffed, feeling the tears she had held at bay so long building in her eyes and clogging her throat.

"Dr. Evans. Emergency room, stat. Dr. Evans. Emergency room, stat."

"Damn," he hissed. "I have to go. I love you. I'll call you as soon as I take care of this." With a quick peck on her cheek, he was racing to the elevator. It opened almost immediately. He waved, then the door closed and he was gone.

"She's after him. I just know it and he won't listen," Christine cried, reaching for another tissue on the coffee table in the family room of her parents' home. She'd thought of going to see her father, but she hadn't wanted to deal with Uncle Eddie and Aunt Etta. Instead she'd driven to her mother.

"I can't believe he actually thought he could kiss me after having that . . . . that . . ." Christine's lips clamped together before the word she wanted to call Loretta slipped out. "I should have snatched her bald."

Denise continued the relentless sweep of her hand up and down Christine's rigid back. There was nothing else she could think of doing to help. It had taken thirty minutes to calm her hot-tempered daughter down enough for her to explain what had upset her. The incident with Reese couldn't have happened at a worse time. Christine had enough to contend with.

"Reese loves you," Denise said.

"That may be, but that's not stopping that woman from trying to take him from me."

After hearing her daughter's account of what had happened, Denise was inclined to agree with her daughter. "Christine, if this woman is—"

"*If!*" Christine cried. "Weren't you listening?"

Since Denise knew exactly how it felt when your marriage was threatened, she didn't reprimand her daughter for her tone. Instead she closed her hand over her daughter's, clamped tightly in her lap. "Please, let me finish. If she is after Reese, and I believe she is, by letting your temper do the talking for you, you left the door wide open for her."

"If he really loved me, no matter what that woman did, he wouldn't look at her twice." Christine turned on the sofa to face her mother. "Daddy would never cheat on you or you on him. Whatever problems you are having, infidelity isn't one of them."

With difficulty Denise kept her hand and voice steady. "We aren't discussing your father's and my problems."

"He loves you."

Not enough or too much, the results are the same. He wants me dependent on him. "Christine."

"All right, but he does."

Denise almost smiled. Christine was loyal to a fault. "It's after twelve. You're not driving home. Call Reese and tell him where you are so he won't worry."

"He won't miss me with Loretta there," Christine

said bitterly but she reached for the phone on the end table by the couch and dialed Reese's cell.

"Dr. Evans," answered a too-sweet female voice.

Christine shot to her feet. "What are you doing answering my husband's phone?" she asked, then seconds later slammed the receiver down. "I should have snatched her bald!"

Denise rose to place a comforting hand on her daughter's rigid arm. "What is it?"

"*She* answered the phone," Christine explained, folding her arms defensively around her stomach. "She said he had lost his cell, but he's too conscientious, I tease him all the time about being surgically attached to it. He never takes it off until he's ready for bed and always puts it back on when he puts his pants back . . ." Her voice trailed off as the implication of her words sunk in. "Mama."

Denise pulled her daughter into her arms. "Don't borrow trouble. Wait until you hear what Reese has to say."

Christine shook her head, her shoulders shaking from the force of her tears.

Denise thought of Edward. Maybe he could help. "Christine, do—"

The phone interrupted her. "That's probably Reese," Denise said, helping Christine to retake a seat on the sofa before picking up the phone. "Hello." Her gaze swung to her daughter, her arms wrapped once again around her stomach. "Reese, yes, she's here. Christine?"

She shook her head.

"She doesn't want to talk. Maybe in the morning," Denise said, feeling sorry for the desperation in Reese's voice and wishing he were a little more perceptive about women. "Reese, we both know how stubborn she can be . . . All right." Denise put the phone to her daughter's ear.

Moments later more tears coursed down Christine's smooth brown cheeks, then she was up and heading for the stairs. Denise brought the receiver back to her face. "Reese, I have to go." Hanging up the phone, Denise followed and found Christine in her old room in her bed, crying her heart out. Denise had kept both the rooms as they'd been if the children ever wanted to spend the night.

Sitting beside her daughter, she stroked Christine's black, shoulder-length hair.

"He said he'd die without me," Christine cried, curled into a knot.

Denise continued stroking her daughter's hair. "Don't give up, Christine."

"What if I don't have a choice? What if he's given up on me?"

For herself Denise knew what the answer was, but this was her child, her only daughter.

"You fight to get him back."

Christine rolled over on her back and looked up at her mother through tear-stained eyes. "Are you going to fight?"

"That's what I'm doing," she said softly, then went on to explain and finished by saying, "Your father has to let me make my own decisions and to stop taking me for granted."

Christine bit her lower lip. "I think we all did."

"I let you because I loved you so much, but I did us all a disservice." Denise's expression hardened. "It stops now."

Christine gazed at her mother with new appreciation. "Mama, I've never seen you like this."

A smile touched Denise's lips. "Neither have I, and to quote Mr. Brown, I feel good."

Eleven

Friday afternoon Denise answered the front door with a smile on her face and laughter flowing from her mauve-colored lips. She'd seen Edward coming up the walk. His timing was perfect. Round three was about to begin.

Edward's gaze locked on her, then zeroed in on the ruggedly handsome man coming down the stairs and continuing into the family room. "Who's that?" he demanded, trying to brush pass Denise.

A sweetly innocent smile on her face, Denise continued to hold the doorknob, effectively blocking his path. "Did you forget something?"

He scowled down at her. "Who's that man?"

Since his left eyelid had begun to twitch, Denise thought it best to answer him, although she was positive he wasn't going to like hearing what she had to say. "Come inside and I'll introduce you."

Edward stalked inside as soon as she stepped back. Quickly shoving the door closed, she hurried after him. She'd forgotten how possessive and jealous Edward had been when they were dating. The man rose from the sofa in the family room, a smile on his darkly handsome face. Denise gave him points for smiling instead of running for the nearest exit as Edward headed for him.

"Edward, this is Paul Carter, the wonderful man who is going to sell our house."

Edward stopped on a dime and whirled toward her. Denise thought it prudent to take a couple of steps back, Edward had never been violent, but he'd never had a tic before either. "Paul, this is my husband, Edward."

Either Paul loved living dangerously or he was used to dealing with angry men. Edward outweighed him by thirty pounds and had more muscles. Paul extended his hand and kept his smile in place. "Glad to meet you, Mr. Morrison. Your wife showed me around your beautiful home already. You've got yourself a very nice place here."

Finally, Edward looked at the realtor instead of her. Grateful for the reprieve, Denise took a seat on the navy blue leather sofa and gracefully crossed her long legs, which Edward had always had a thing for. If and when Edward stopped glowering and took a seat across from her, she wanted him to notice she wore a cranberry-colored, figure-flattering knit dress.

"This house shouldn't stay on the market very long," Paul said, sitting beside her. "It's even lovelier and more appealing on the inside than on the outside."

"Thank you," Denise said, thinking it was fortuitous that Christine had a realtor friend who didn't mind helping with Denise's plan. "It's nice of you to come out so quickly. I just called Wednesday."

Paul flashed her a set of perfect white teeth. She thought she heard Edward growl. "Your home is in a very desirable area. Peachtree Crossing has excellent schools, is near the expressway and, despite the growth of the surrounding area, has managed to keep the close-knit neighborhood feel." His manicured hand gestured around the living area. She caught the flash of his gold Rolex. "Buyers will snap this one up fast. You have so much space and the house is so well laid out."

"My husband built the house," Denise commented, the pride coming through in her voice as she looked at the high-ceilinged room with crown molding and inserts, the hardwood floors, the bay window that was repeated in the separate dining room across the hall. They'd planned the house for years before they actually had the money to build and by then they'd had a boxful of ideas.

"*We* built this house," Edward stated with pointed emphasis.

Her gaze met his. He wasn't looking at her with anger any longer. In his face she saw traces of the loving, wonderful man she had begun falling in love with the instant she'd first seen him.

Paul nodded, then made a notation in his notebook. "You did a marvelous job. The house flows beautifully, and is picture perfect. Did you have a decorator?"

"I did everything myself," Denise said, picking up a pillow covered in pale blue damask that exactly matched the covering of the Queen Anne side chair. "Of course, I had nothing to do with *that* chair."

The realtor's gaze followed the direction of Denise's. His expression became pained as he stared at the orange tweed chair. He cleared his throat. "You might consider placing it in the garage. It throws off the aesthetic flow and beauty of the room."

"Nobody touches my chair," Edward snarled.

Paul blinked, drawing his notebook closer to his chest. Perhaps he wasn't as immune to Edward as she had thought.

"I'll certainly take your suggestion into consideration," Denise placated, urging the realtor to continue.

Paul nodded, then glanced around again and

made another notation. "I assume you plan to leave the custom draperies throughout the house?"

"Of course." She'd spent countless hours searching for the right fabric in the right colors at the right price, then more hours sewing. She'd wanted to make their home a place her family could be proud of. She'd succeeded in that, if not in making her family proud of her.

Once again her gaze fell on the side chair that a stiff Edward sat even more stiffly in. It had been a garage sale find that they had refinished, and she'd reupholstered. She'd been so scared of wasting the fabric she'd caught on sale at a fraction of the original price, but Edward had said if anybody could do it, she could. He'd always been supportive of whatever she did in the house, but when it came to the children or their finances he always made the final decisions.

Her short, oval nails dug into the pillow. He had no confidence in her if she wasn't cooking or sewing.

"Excellent." Putting the notebook aside, the realtor pulled a clipboard with a form attached from his briefcase. "Now, all I need is the both of your signatures on this sales agreement. I plan to put your house on our website and feature it prominently. We should get hits right away."

"I'm not signing," Edward said, his voice defiant.

Denise paused in reaching for the clipboard. She studied her husband's hard expression for a moment, then turned to Paul. "Why don't you leave the papers and you can pick them up when they're signed?"

Paul needed no further urging. He practically threw the sales agreement at Denise as he gathered his things and made a hasty retreat to the front door. "Thank you, again."

Feeling Edward's gaze boring a hole in the middle of her back, Denise said, "Thank you for coming."

"My pleasure." Paul glanced up at the crystal chandelier above in the vaulted ceiling, then back at Denise. "And please rest assured that Homestead Realtors prides itself on only bringing serious clients to see properties. We respect our clients' privacy, which is another reason we don't put up signs in the yards."

"I appreciate that." Denise was glad she had thought of that potential problem. She had a couple of nosy neighbors who would be all in her affairs if they had a hint of what was going on. This was family business.

"Good-bye. I hope to have a prospective buyer out within the week, and when you're ready to look for a place of your own, I'm at your disposal. I have some simply gorgeous condos in my listings."

Denise heard that growl again. She discreetly shooed Paul out the door. "Good-bye."

"Good-bye." After a friendly nod, he went down the curved walk to the gleaming black Mercedes sports utility vehicle parked by the curb. Denise waited until he got inside the car before turning and facing her angry husband.

"I can't believe you'd really sell the house!"

"It's too big for either of us to care for alone," she said, brushing by him and going to the kitchen for a glass of water. She wished she could add an aspirin for the headache that was building, but that might be too revealing. In the past she'd always shied away from confrontations.

Opening the oak cabinet and seeing the jumble of glasses increased the pain in her head. Edward and the children—she doubted his aunt and uncle had helped—had washed the dishes and cleaned up the kitchen last night. Since they never helped, they had stuck things where there was room and not where they went. It had taken her ten minutes this morning to find the skillet to fix Christine's breakfast.

She was just annoyed enough to turn and glare at her husband. "Look what you did!"

He blinked. "What are you talking about?"

"This." Her hand gestured wildly toward the glasses. "My cabinets below are even worse."

He crept closer as if he expected something to jump out and bite him. He peered at the glasses, then back at her. "What?"

Denise bit back a frustrated scream and started pulling glasses out. "They're supposed to be grouped by design and size."

"Oh," he mumbled.

Denise continued until she felt his warm hand on her arm. Startled, she glanced up at him.

"I messed it up. I'll do it."

She simply stared at him. If her family wasn't eating, they didn't want to be anywhere near the kitchen.

He stared back. "I can do it."

"Be my guest," she said and went to the refrigerator. If Christine returned after work, Denise wanted dinner ready. Hopefully, she'd eat this time. She'd picked over her favorite breakfast of strawberry waffles.

Denise hoped Christine had followed her advice to talk to Reese again, and try to listen without losing her temper. The thought of her daughter going through what she was experiencing made her entire body ache.

Last night had been the worst in her life. She hadn't been able to go to sleep until almost dawn. She and Edward had always slept cuddled together. They might not start out that way, but always, always, before the night was over, she'd find her head pillowed on his chest, his arm draped possessively around her shoulders, keeping her close. She had wakened to the steady beat of his heart for over half her life. Now he was gone and the loss left her feeling empty and strangely adrift. If she couldn't take three nights, how was she going to get her plan to work?

"Why didn't you call me last night when Christine came back?"

If he had sounded accusatory instead of worried, she might not have answered. "There was nothing you could do. I called you this morning."

He paused with a crystal goblet in his hand, then nodded. "I couldn't get her at work so I decided to come over. Is she coming back here?"

Denise bit her bottom lip and hugged her arms around her waist. "I don't know. She told me she wouldn't call today because she would be in meetings. She was miserable when she left his morning. It tears me up, seeing her in pain."

"Dee, don't," he said and started toward her.

She wanted him to take her in his arms, wanted to accept the comfort of his arms, and it might have happened if the doorbell hadn't rung. In an instant, Edward's handsome face hardened.

"That better not be that realtor guy."

Denise quickly pulled herself together. That had been a little too close. "He has no reason to come back." Passing him, she tossed over her shoulder,

"When you finish the glasses, the pots and pans under the cabinet need your attention as well."

He grunted.

Smiling, Denise continued to the front, then she opened the door and her smile vanished. Anthony, his head downcast, his hands shoved into the pockets of his slacks, stood on the doorstep. Guilt stabbed her. She hadn't meant to hurt her children.

"Baby." She gathered him into her arms before she remembered that he had stopped wanting her to hug him in the fifth grade. He'd been too big for that. As his arms closed tightly around her, she was glad he'd forgotten as well.

"Come into the kitchen. There's pecan and chocolate pie," she said, pulling him inside, hoping his favorite desserts would cheer him up.

"I'm not hungry," he said, finally lifting his head.

Her worry increased on seeing the despair and uncertainty in his eyes. "Anthony, please don't worry about your father and me."

"I can't help it. If you and Dad can't make it, who can?" Anthony asked, closing the door behind him.

Denise's gaze sharpened on her son, the carefree playboy. *My baby*. "Are you getting serious about Sherri?"

The horrified expression on his face was so comical she almost laughed. "No. I like Sherri, but jeez, Mama, I'm only twenty-one. I'm young yet."

She refrained from reminding him that Christine was a year old when her father was twenty-one. Edward had shouldered the heavy responsibility without grumbling a single time. He'd gotten up in the middle of the night during her pregnancy on several occasions to go across town and get her strawberry pie from the twenty-four-hour diner. He would come back home and tease her about keeping both of his ladies happy. They'd somehow known it would be a girl. Now, looking at her son, Denise couldn't imagine him shouldering the responsibility of a family. She still did his laundry.

"It's probably just as well." She tucked her arm through his. "Come on into the kitchen. Your father dropped by to see Christine."

They both halted in the doorway on seeing the cooking utensils on the floor surrounding Edward. "Hi, Daddy, what happened?"

"Hello, son. I was trying to straighten them out." Edward sat cross-legged amid the chaos. "Pull off your coat and give me a hand. Maybe your mother will take pity on you and feed you."

"I offered; he isn't hungry," she said.

Anthony slipped his hands out of his pockets. "On second thought, I guess I am a little hungry."

Denise shared a smile with her husband. *He'd always claimed Anthony had a hollow leg.* Then, becoming aware of the intimacy of their shared thought, she flushed and looked away. "I better get back to fixing dinner."

"Do you need anything from under here?" Edward asked, then frowned. "You need a pull-out shelf under here."

Denise, who had been looking at Edward, saw him stiffen. She knew he had remembered that they were putting the house on the market. Suddenly she wanted to reach out to him, to hold and reassure him as he had done for her so many times in the past, but she couldn't. "The kitchen is fine the way it is." Turning away, she reached into the drawer for her carving knife. "Have you eaten?"

"No," came Edward's quiet answer.

"He didn't eat his lunch today," Anthony volunteered as he removed his jacket and dropped down beside his father. "I went by his office."

He hadn't eaten last night either, Denise thought. She knew she had said he was on his own, but it was *her* plan, and she was allowed to change the rules. "I'll fix enough for all of us. There's turkey and ham." Usually there wasn't enough left to make a sandwich after her family snacked all through the football games and his aunt and uncle took food home.

Just as she clicked on the electric knife the doorbell rang.

"I'll get it." Anthony straightened and headed for the front door.

Denise stared after her fast retreating son, then shook her head. "He's always been quick when it comes to getting out of housework."

"Yeah," Edward said, placing a broiler beneath the cabinet. "Guess I wasn't much help either. I didn't know where half this stuff went."

"It doesn't matter." She turned back to the turkey and clicked on the knife.

"I'm not signing the papers, Dee," he said quietly.

Denise whirled around, shutting off the knife as she did. Hope spiraled through her. She tried to look outraged instead of happy. He was going to fight for her and their marriage. "You have to. We agreed."

"I never thought you'd go through with it." He stood with the same agile grace as his son, and came to her. "I don't want to lose the house, or you."

Her spirits plummeted. Even now he put the house first. He just wanted his orderly life back, "You promised, and I'm holding you to it."

"You better carve some more turkey, Mama."

Denise glanced around to see Christine, her eyes red and puffy, a suitcase in her hand. Denise reached her daughter seconds before Edward. "Christine, what is it?"

"C-can I stay here for a few days?" she asked between sobs.

Denise's heart sank. Her gaze went to Edward and saw his tight-lipped expression. He hurt for their daughter as much as she did. "Of course. I'll take your bag and go up with you."

Christine shook her head of long, straight hair. "No. I just want to be by myself for a bit."

"Pumpkin," Edward began, then sighed. "You're sure this is what you want to do?"

Christine brushed a tear away with the heel of her hand. "I wasn't given much choice in the matter."

Before Denise could ask her to explain, Christine turned and started from the room. Anthony stared after her.

"See that your sister gets to her room all right. I don't want her tripping on the stairs."

"Sure, Mama. This Christmas season is the pits," Anthony said, then followed his sister.

Denise's arms circled her waist. "What's happening? Christine's life is unraveling and there is nothing I can do about it. What I've done is just causing her more pain."

"Dee, don't." Edward pulled her gently into his arms.

She thought of resisting, but she badly needed the comfort of his arms. "I feel like this is somehow my fault."

Gently he pushed her from him and stared down into her tortured face. "I hate like hell that you want to leave me and what I thought was a good marriage, but I won't let you take the blame for what's happening to Christine. You're a good mother, Denise." He brushed her hair back in an old familiar gesture of affection he hadn't used in years. "That's why I could pull the long hours trying to get the business off the ground, because I knew you were here with the children and I didn't have to worry."

Her eyes widened in shock. "Y-you never complimented me before about the children."

He frowned. "I must have. All the things you do for us. It's impossible that I didn't tell you how I felt."

"She made it upstai—" Anthony's voice stopped abruptly.

Oddly embarrassed at being caught in her husband's arms, Denise pulled away. "Thank you, Anthony."

Busying herself with putting the turkey in the oven, she tried to ignore the warm feeling created by Edward's compliment, which made her feel almost as good as being in his arms again. Maybe, just maybe, her plan was working, even if it was killing her to go through with it.

Twelve

Edward eased past his aunt and uncle's bedroom door in the hope that he could get to his room without letting them know he was home. The last thing he needed was another lecture from his uncle about his husbandly duties, or a scolding from his aunt about his bedtime. The floorboards squeaked and he held his breath. He felt like a kid sneaking in after curfew.

Finding Paul, or whatever his name was, in his house, smiling at his wife, had really done a number on his head. He was more upset about his presence than the idea that Denise was trying to sell the house right out from under all of them.

The jolly green giant had kicked in and he felt like doing the same to Mr. Perfect Teeth's teeth. "Probably caps," he grumbled.

He went into the bathroom, hoping that a nice hot

bath would soothe his body and his mind. As he watched the steamy water fill the tub, he thought about the many nights and mornings that he and Denise had shared a bath together. Even after all these years, she still turned him on. The touch of her skin beneath his fingertips was enough to get his blood boiling. From the moment he'd met Denise, he knew that she was the one for him. He wanted to do for her what his father had been unable to do for his mother. But it seemed that all of his efforts and all of his good intentions had been for nothing. Denise didn't want him in her life anymore and she didn't want anything he had to offer.

Well, he decided, then and there, he was not going to be like his father. He was not going to walk away from everything he loved. Maybe it *was* some kind of "spell" that Denise was going through, like Uncle Eddie had said. But he was going to break the spell and what he needed was some help.

He quickly finished what should have been a leisurely bath, donned the robe that hung on the hook behind the door, and darted off to his room. But he nearly leaped out of his skin when he opened the door to find his aunt and uncle sitting on the bed waiting for him.

"'Bout time, boy," Uncle Eddie announced. "It's past me and Etta's bedtime."

"But what are—"

"I think it's about time we had a talk with you, son," Aunt Etta said.

"That's right. Now, have a sit down and listen."

"Uncle Eddie, if this is going to be another lecture about me coming in after nine—"

"You gonna listen, or run your mouth? That's why you're in the predicament you're in today," Etta admonished. "Now, you do as your uncle told ya."

"Yes, ma'am," he muttered sheepishly. Slowly, Edward took a seat on the hard wooden chair with the bad leg. It rocked a few times, then settled.

Etta took her husband's hand. "Go head, Ed, talk to the boy."

"Seems to me, boy, that you've gotten yourself into a real fix with your wife."

Etta nodded in agreement.

"She done put you out of the house and wants a divorce." He shook his head. "Now, it's not that we don't want you here. It's nice having you back. But to be truthful . . . you're cramping our style . . . if you know what I mean." He winked and Etta giggled.

"Now, you can stay if that's what you really have a mind to do," Etta said. "But a husband's place is at his wife's side. I know you just think we're two old eccentric codgers, but we haven't been together this long by luck."

"I may act the fool," Eddie admitted, "but so does she."

Etta popped him good-naturedly in the arm.

"Ow, woman!"

"Oh, hush. I ain't done nothin' yet."

"I got somethin' for ya in the next room."

"We'll just have to see now, won't we?" Etta said, her voice dropping to a seductive low that made Edward blush.

But what Edward saw beneath all the craziness, nutty antics, and talk of Wild Irish Rose and James Brown records was an unwavering love that radiated between them like lights on a Christmas tree. Maybe it didn't seem like they got along, but they did. They were a team—equals.

Then it hit him like a ton of bricks. That's what Denise had been talking about all along! Equality, being a full partner in the marriage. And he had been so wrapped up in being *the man*, he'd forgotten about being a husband.

Eddie leaned over and kissed his wife on the lips, not caring that they weren't alone, but just needing to show her that he cared, and Edward saw his aunt's eyes light up with joy, the way Denise's eyes used to light up for him.

It was true that his aunt and uncle didn't have the great big, pretty house, two cars, and a six-figure income. But they had something more important—each other.

Eddie took Etta's hand and stood. "Hope you know you can't win her back by sitting on your hands, boy."

"That girl loves you, son," Etta said, brushing his cheek with the palm of her hand.

"You really think so?" Edward asked, needing reassurance.

"I see it in her eyes every time she looks at you. Just imagine, if you don't fix what's ailing in your marriage, you'll be living here with us!" She cackled at her own humor.

"Come on, woman. It's way past this boy's bedtime."

"And ours."

Eddie patted her bottom as they walked out, but not before Etta issued her closing comment.

"The same thing you did to get her is what you need to keep her." She closed the door gently behind them.

In bed that night, Edward thought about his odd counseling session with his aunt and uncle, even as he listened to "Sex Machine" and the bump and grind of their bed against his wall. If they could make their crazy marriage work, so could he. What he needed was a plan. And that plan would begin tomorrow.

Morning couldn't get there fast enough. He'd have to get the help of his son and William, too, but it could be done. He put the pillow over his head to drown out the noise, and smiled.

It was a shame that he had to come up with an excuse to visit his own house, but he knew his wife. She would want to know why he wasn't at work. Well, he already had a story concocted.

Before he headed to his house, he made a pit stop at his son's apartment. He knew it was early, but he wanted to catch Anthony before he got on with his day. He just hoped he wouldn't walk in on anything other than his son.

He jogged up the short flight of stone steps that led to the townhouse where Anthony lived and rang the bell. Moments later his son appeared at the door, showered, dressed, and ready to face the world.

"Hey, Dad." He looked past his father to the lane behind him. "What's up? Is something wrong? You never just drop by."

"Can I come in? I need to talk to you, son."

"*Son*. Hmmm, this sounds serious. Sure, come on in. I have a few minutes."

"I'm not disturbing you, am I?" Edward asked, looking around at the apartment that could certainly use a woman's touch.

Every outfit that Anthony had worn for the past week and maybe longer could be found in various locations throughout the one-bedroom apartment. Empty containers of Chinese food and pizza boxes were lined up on the kitchen counter and on the living room table. If Denise ever saw this, she would have a natural fit. It was no wonder Anthony never invited them over.

"No, you're not disturbing me at all. Excuse the mess. I usually take my clothes over to the house for Mom to put in the laundry or drop off at the cleaners, but . . . with everything going on . . ." His voice drifted off and he looked expectantly at his father. "How are things with you two? You are going to work it out, aren't you, Dad?"

"That's why I'm here." He pushed aside a pile of clothes on the couch and sat down. "I need your help and your advice."

"Me?" Anthony's dark eyes widened with surprise. To have his father come to him suddenly made him feel ten feet tall. For the most part, the family always looked at him as the baby of the family, the one that needed looking after. No one ever asked his opinion or advice on anything of importance. So, it became easy, second nature, to play the role of the needy one, the comic relief. But now his Dad needed him and he was ready to rise to the challenge.

He took a seat opposite his father. "Sure, Dad, whatever you need."

Edward leaned forward. "Okay . . . here's the plan . . ."

Thirteen

Denise was nursing a cup of coffee when the doorbell rang Monday morning. She ignored it. Thoughts about Christine filled her mind. Her daughter hadn't said one word about what had happened since she had arrived Friday night with a suitcase. Thirty minutes ago she had left for work without even a hint of what had happened to send her running back home in tears.

Denise might have pushed if her daughter hadn't looked so miserable, hadn't spent most of her time in her room. Both had stayed home from church Sunday. Denise couldn't honestly say if she stayed for Christine's sake—in case she needed her—or if she was trying to protect them both. There was bound to be talk once the parishioners saw Christine's red eyes and woebegone expression. Even more eyebrows would be raised on seeing that Denise and Edward weren't sitting together. He rarely worked on Sunday and they generally attended church services together.

Taking a sip of her coffee, Denise wondered if he had gone by himself. She hadn't wanted to ask when he had come by briefly yesterday afternoon. He had tried to talk to Christine and had been met with the same polite refusal she had given Denise.

The doorbell sounded again. With a heavy sigh, Denise placed the heavy yellow stoneware mug on the tiled counter and stood. Whoever it was, wasn't going away.

Opening the door, she was surprised, then worried, to see Edward standing there with a frown on his face. "Has something else happened?"

"No," he quickly said, reaching out to gently touch her arm in reassurance.

It ran through Denise's mind that he had touched her more in the last few days than in months. "Then why were you frowning?"

He sent her a self-conscious grin. "I thought you had gone to the grocery store or something and you weren't here."

"I do the grocery shopping on Mondays, but not until later," she told him, thinking how far their marriage had disintegrated that he didn't know that simple fact about her household schedule for the past fifteen years.

Edward sighed and shoved his hands into the pockets of his jeans. "I should know that, shouldn't I?"

"You're busy," she said. Despite everything, he loved his children and worked hard. He just didn't need her.

He studied her closely for a few moments, then said, "Can I come in?"

"Of course," she said. Flustered, she stepped back. "I'm sorry, I wasn't thinking. Would you like a cup of coffee?"

"If it's not too much trouble?"

For some odd reason, Denise felt tears sting her eyes. They were so formal and distant. Resolutely she continued to the kitchen. She just had to believe that things would work out.

"You're doing all right, Dee?" he asked.

His nickname for her caused more tears to sting her eyes. "Of course."

"Don't worry about the children. They'll be all right," he said, following her into the bright kitchen.

She took the out he gave her. "Christine won't tell me why she came back home." Taking down another mug, she filled it with coffee and automatically added two tablespoons of sugar and a dollop of condensed milk. She turned and paused in surprise. Edward was sitting on the barstool at the end of the counter, where she'd been sitting. Once she would have welcomed him there, but now she wasn't so sure.

Setting his cup in front of him, she picked up her own cup and remained standing. "Reese didn't call as he did at Thanksgiving. They were supposed to visit his parents this past weekend."

Edward's large, long-fingered hands circled the mug of steaming coffee. For just a moment she stared at the hands, whose palms were ringed with calluses but had always touched her with aching tenderness and endless love.

"That doesn't sound too good," Edward said.

"I know," she admitted, coming out of her daze to lean a slim hip against the edge of the counter. "She kept glancing at the phone while picking at her breakfast this morning. I think she might regret her decision, but she's too full of pride and stubbornness to admit she might have overreacted."

"Pride makes for a cold bedmate."

The deep timbre of his voice, the sudden intensity of his eyes, had her hand tightening on the cup, her heat thumping in her chest. Only Edward had the power to awaken passion in her. Had he missed her as much as she had missed him? She brought the unwanted and now cold coffee to her mouth. It was too late for second thoughts. "Christine is hurting."

He nodded. "Families should be happy and to-gether, especially during the Christmas holidays."

Denise refused to rise to the bait and continued sipping her coffee.

"You think I should talk to Reese?" he asked in the lengthening silence.

Denise blinked. "You're asking me?"

Lines of confusion radiated across his strong forehead. "Yeah. You and he always seemed to get along, and he's a lot like Anthony."

Edward's observation was on the money, but the last time they had discussed a family matter was when they were building the house twenty years ago. Did he really want her opinion or was he say-ing what he thought she wanted to hear? Denise studied his open expression and decided to give him the benefit of the doubt. "I think we both should let them work this out on their own. Chris-tine is worried about this woman, but if she isn't careful she'll push Reese right into that nurse's arms."

"You're going to talk to her?" he asked.

"What about you?" she asked, deciding to test his sincerity. He was always the one the children ran to. They deferred to him in all things.

He shook his dark head. "I couldn't get a peep out of her yesterday. She came to you both times."

"She came to a place where she had always been loved and protected."

"Exactly," Edward said. "And you have always been here to give her whatever she needed."

No, it was you, Denise thought, but it went no further. She was here now for her daughter and she'd walk through hell to help her. "I'll do whatever it takes."

"Then I won't worry." Standing, he drained the coffee cup and set it down.

Denise saw the way he looked at her, with complete confidence, and felt almost light-headed. "I'll keep in touch to let you know how she's doing."

"You need anything?" He continued to stare down at her.

Looks like I'm getting what I need. "No. I'm fine."

He nodded, his reluctance to leave obvious. "Thanks for the coffee. I better get going. I'm already late to the office."

Denise glanced at her watch as she followed him to the door. It was 9:15. "You never go in this late. Is everything all right?"

He sighed in irritation. "Fine. I forgot to put my jeans in the dryer last night and had to go buy a pair."

Denise looked at the new jeans that encased his long, muscular legs and tight butt, and gave her own sigh of regret that she'd be sleeping alone tonight. "I hope you bought an extra pair in case it happens again."

His eyes narrowed as if he hadn't expected that reply. "Yeah." Then, as if he couldn't hold it back any longer, he said, "I miss you, Dee. I love you."

"Or do you love your orderly life? Are you willing to let me run mine?"

"Is this about you sewing for people?" he asked, his look accusing.

Hands on her slim hips, she stared right back. "It's about you seeing and treating me as your wife and partner, not housekeeper, cook, and bedmate."

"You enjoy our lovemaking as much as I do," he said, catching her arms and pulling her against his hard body. "If you want to go upstairs, I can give you a demonstration."

Wrenching her arm free, she jabbed her finger into his wide chest. "Did you hear yourself? You completely glazed over the first two things I said and jumped to sex. And who said it always had to be in the bedroom?"

His eyes bugged. "Dee!"

Seeing him off guard, she pulled away, walked to the front door, and opened it. "As I said, I'll keep you informed on how things go with Christine."

"Dee?"

She stared at the white silk draperies in the bay

window in the living room. "Edward, you have to leave or I'll be late for an appointment."

"I'm going, but I'll be back," he said stubbornly.

Denise watched him slowly walk down the sidewalk toward the SUV parked at the curb. Against her will, she noticed again the width of his broad shoulders beneath the suede coat, the enticing way the blue denim cupped his butt, his long, muscular legs. A sigh fluttered over her lips. She felt a quickening deep inside her body. It had been almost a week since they had been intimate.

Edward climbed inside the vehicle and drove away. Denise closed the door, trying to get her mind on anything but Edward's body joining with hers. He was right; he had always known just how to please her.

But so was she. They'd christened every room in the house during that first year.

Her gaze strayed to the carpeted area in front of the bay window. She could almost see them there after the children had gone to bed. They had been in the house less than a month. Edward had had an expensive bottle of wine, a couple of candles, and chocolate-covered strawberries. They'd been insatiable. He could love her body, he just had to respect her mind as well. And before she was through with him, he would.

Fourteen

When Edward was sure he was out of Denise's line of sight, he pulled to the curb and thought about what she'd said. How could she think he took making love to her for granted or used it as an excuse to gloss over their problems? Making love to his wife made everything right with the world. It replenished him and he thought it showed her the depths of his feelings for her. It was obvious that although his intentions were good, the true meaning was lost somehow. Well, if she truly needed to be shown that she was number one in his life, he planned to do whatever it took—even if it meant keeping his raging libido in check. As for their daughter, he honestly believed that what Christine needed now was her mother's touch, as much as he wanted to butt in and protect his baby girl. Maybe that too would assure Denise that her presence, her opinion, and her help were still needed with their children. He'd been an idiot not to have realized it eons ago. He took out his cell phone and dialed Anthony at his office.

"How did it go?" Anthony asked the moment he saw his father's cell number on the caller ID. He swiveled his seat so that his back was to the opening of his cubicle, giving him a semblance of privacy.

"So far so good," Edward said, leaving out the intimate details, of course. "Did you get your stuff together?"

"All done. I'll call Mom around lunchtime. I'll dart over to my place when I get off work, then on to the homestead."

"Great. I'll be at the office if you need me."

"Can you get phone calls after nine?" Anthony asked, then cracked up laughing.

"Very funny," Edward growled. "This won't last too much longer, I can guarantee that. Your mom has given me plenty to think about, but I want her to do some thinking too."

"Dad, I know I didn't say this earlier, but . . . you putting your faith in me and confiding in me really means a lot."

There was a poignant silence between father and son.

"Knowing that I can turn to you means a lot as well, son," Edward finally said.

There was a rally of throat clearing.

"Well, I guess I better get back to work," Anthony

said. "I'll call you on your cell if anything goes wrong."

"I don't see how it could. If there's one thing I know about your mom, she won't let anything happen to her kids."

"That's true. She's like those lionesses in *National Geographic*. She may lurk in the background, but she's always ready to protect her cubs."

Edward smiled. Yes, Denise was all that and more. It was the "more" that he'd been too blind to see all these years. Being away from her helped him to realize what a fool he'd been. But his eyes were wide open now. He was going to prove to her that she was the center of his life, that they would be happier with each other than without, and he would battle his old ideals and demons if it meant keeping his wife and family intact. However, in the meantime, he had a trick or two up his sleeve.

"Well, Dad, I'll check in later," Anthony said, cutting into Edward's thoughts. He laughed. "You know what this reminds me of?"

"What's that, son?"

"Plotting with my boys to get the attention of some chick."

Edward's eyebrows rose. "Some chick?"

Anthony flinched. "Uh, young lady."

Edward chuckled. "I'd better get to work. We'll talk later."

"Roger that."

Edward shook his head and ended the call with the touch of a button. Anthony was really getting into this. Funny, but even as traumatic as this whole situation was, it brought him closer to his son. He'd always had a special relationship with Christine, "Daddy's little girl," but he'd never developed that real closeness with Anthony. He'd gravitated toward his mother, who gave him everything he wanted, just as Denise did for him. As a result they'd both taken all she did for them for granted. That was all about to change. But . . . in the meantime, he would have to use the old rules and old habits to his advantage, at least for now.

"Well, darling, I hope you know what you started," he said aloud with a wicked smile before pulling off and heading to work. "Now for step two."

It was hard for Edward to concentrate on the tasks at hand in his office. Lena had a million pieces of paper for him to read and sign off on. But his mind was on getting his wife back. It was a little more than three weeks before Christmas arrived and he had no intention of spending it under the roof of his aunt and uncle!

Edward checked the clock that hung above his

door. It was almost noon. William was scheduled to return from his meeting downtown any minute. He'd left word with Lena to send him in as soon as he arrived.

He flipped open his sketch pad and looked at the design that he'd been working on since last night. It was perfect. What made it great was that the entire layout would be prefabricated. A few nails, anchors, and fancy footwork and it would be done. With William's help he figured the whole job should take about two to three days tops. The trick was it would have to be completed without anyone knowing what they were doing. He added a few more touches to the design just as there was a knock on his door.

"Come in."

"Hey, man. Lena said you wanted to see me. What's up? Everything okay with the job site?"

"Yeah, yeah. Come on in and close the door." He waited for William to take a seat. "Listen, remember the day of the groundbreaking?"

William nodded, his expression pinching in concern. "Did something happen?"

"No." Edward cleared his throat and looked uncomfortable for a moment. Opening himself up was never something that he'd been good at; confessing his feelings or troubles to anyone, especially to another man, went against everything that made him who he was. But he also realized that if he was to accomplish what he set out to do, he was going to have to change. He took a deep breath.

"The day of the groundbreaking you asked me if everything was all right at home. Well . . . everything is not all right at home. And hasn't been for a long time . . . at least according to Denise. She decided to teach me a lesson."

"A lesson?"

"She asked for a divorce."

"Aw, Ed, I'm really sorry. You and Denise . . . I can't believe it."

"Neither can I. And I don't believe that she wants it any more than I do. But for the time being I'm staying at my aunt and uncle's house."

"Eddie and Etta?" he asked with alarm, knowing how loony those two were and how they drove Edward crazy.

"Yeah, and trust me, it hasn't been fun." He shook his head. "Those two might be nutty as fruitcakes as Anthony would say, but I learned something since I've been there. Watching them, for all of their antics, they are a team, something that Denise and I haven't been for a long time. I had this crazy notion that I could do it all, be 'the man.' That's not what makes a marriage work. It takes two. This has been a marriage of one for a long time. Denise had been trying to tell me, but I wasn't listening. I just figured as long as I took care of everything, paid all the bills, and kept my nose clean, that was all that was necessary. And that's how it's been for a long time. I don't intend to let it stay that way. I want her to know that I'm finally listening." He paused for a moment. "I need your help."

William leaned forward, bracing his arms on his thighs. "Hey, man, anything I can do to help."

Edward smiled, and a slow sensation of relief filled him. He thought it would be hard unburdening himself, but maybe that's what he needed to do all along, just as his wife had done. There was so much that he needed to tell her and he didn't believe that when he did it would make him any less the man he should be.

"I was hoping you'd say that. Well . . . here's the deal . . ."

Edward laid out his plan in detail and all the supplies and equipment that he would need. Finished, he leaned back and waited for William's reaction.

"Wow." He grinned. "If she doesn't take you back with arms wide open after this, I'll take her place," he joked.

Edward laughed. "I don't think so, my man. I spent one night with you and that was enough to last a lifetime. I don't see how your wife can stand it."

William feigned hurt. "But I make up for it in very creative ways." He winked.

The two men slapped five.

"I hear ya," Edward said. "So, do you think we can pull this off in time?"

"Without a doubt."

"I want you to start gathering up the supplies. Keep a strict inventory. I'll cover it from my personal account."

"How are we going to manage to pull this off without anyone finding out?"

"I'll handle that. Keep your cell phone on you and not in the car. Every time there's an opening, I'm going to need you to be ready. Anthony has everything else covered."

"Tony?" William grinned.

"He's really stepped up to the plate. I guess I underestimated him too."

"Hey, sometimes all folks need is a good reason and they rise to the occasion."

Edward nodded slowly in agreement. "Exactly. And I have a damned good one."

Fifteen

How much do you love Reese?" Denise asked that night at dinner and watched as Christine, seated next to her, tensed, her fingers clenching on her fork.

Christine had come home from work an hour ago, as uncommunicative and miserable as when she had left. She'd cut her smothered pork chop into tiny pieces and had then proceeded to push the meat around on her plate for the past five minutes.

When no answer came, Denise decided drastic measures were required. "Are you just going to let that woman have him?"

That brought Christine's head up. Her brown eyes glittered with as much pain as anger. "He doesn't believe me. The more I say, the more he defends her. He keeps insisting they're only friends since he was in med school."

"Reese, unfortunately like most men, can be naïve and gullible at times. They hear us talking, but not a word we say," Denise said, recalling her own experience with Edward.

"Exactly." Christine plunked her fork on the plate. "He kept defending her, telling me how immature I was. Then . . . then . . ." Her hands clenched.

Denise waited. Christine's temper was awesome when it erupted.

"That she-devil called not five minutes later and told me the bald-faced lie that she had no interest in my husband, and sprouted that same lie about being just friends, the same put-down that I wasn't being 'mature.' How could he have discussed me with that woman!"

"Men can be fools!" Denise said without a moment's hesitation. Edward was a prime example.

Christine blinked, then burst into tears. "But I still love him."

"I love your daddy too," Denise said. Rising, she went to her daughter and pulled her into her arms. "This may be hard to hear, but if you want him, crying is not going to help you get him back."

"I could pull her weave out."

"As satisfying as that sounds, it won't make Reese realize that she's after him or get you two back together." Denise rubbed Christine's back and appealed to her fighting spirit. "You didn't answer my question. Are you just going to give up on him or are you going to show that woman she can't mess with your man?"

Sniffing, Christine lifted her head. "You seem to have Daddy's attention, but I don't know what to do about Reese."

"Sometimes I wonder about your daddy," Denise said, then shook her head and continued. "But let's talk about you. I have an idea. I watched enough talk shows to learn a few things about the inconsistency of men. First, Reese, just like your daddy, needs a dose of reality to appreciate what he has in you. Your daddy was so jealous of your realtor friend he almost had a stroke. I'll just bet Reese would act the same way at the first hint of another man taking an interest in you. That nurse may be looking at him, but he needs to realize that other men might be looking at you."

Christine scrubbed her face, then looked thoughtful. "He did act jealous when I asked him how he would feel if he caught me kissing a doctor on his rotation."

"Perfect." Denise gestured for her daughter to continue her meal. "We'll strategize while we eat."

Christine picked up her fork, then glanced at her mother for reassurance. "You think it will work?"

Denise covered her daughter's free hand. It had been a long time since Christine had come to her for advice or assurance. She wasn't going to let her down. "Reese loves you, but unfortunately, men often become complacent with what they are assured of."

"Is that what happened with you and Daddy?"

Denise sat back in her chair. "Yes. Your father was busy building his business and I was busy with you, Anthony, and this house. We didn't take the time for each other."

"Daddy is miserable without you."

Denise smiled sadly. "I feel the same way, but if I want us to have the kind of marriage we once had, I have to play this out. Good marriages just don't happen. Love is a start, but you have to build on it and keep building. A coal will burn longer if you stoke it once in a while, otherwise it dies."

Christine grinned. "Is that what we're going to do?"

Denise grinned back. "You bet." She took a bite of her pork chop. "I seem to remember you and Reese were going to a Christmas dance Saturday night."

The happiness left Christine's face. "I had intended to buy a new dress, but I don't see the point now."

"The point is you're going to take your husband back," Denise told her. "I'll make you a gown that will make him salivate."

Christine blinked, then giggled. "Mama!"

Taking a bite of her smothered pork chops, Denise was pleased to see Christine do the same. "That woman doesn't have anything you don't, and in the creation I'm going to design and make for you, Reese will be able to see that very well."

"Oh, my goodness." Christine had to put her hand over her mouth full of food. "I've never seen you like this."

"No one threatens my family. No one."

"Do you think we could start with the design tonight?" Christine's eyes gleamed as she buttered her roll.

"As soon as I finish the kitchen," Denise answered, relieved and thankful her daughter no longer wore that unhappy, defeated expression.

"I'll help. We can get through faster, and we can talk more strategy," Christine said with a pleased smile. "I should have talked to you when I was dating."

"I'm here now," Denise said quietly.

Christine paused in reaching for her tea glass. She looked at her mother. "I'm glad that you are."

"Me, too," Denise said, feeling a lightness of spirit she hadn't felt in a long time.

Feeling good about her daughter, Denise phoned Edward after she retired for the night. As they talked she realized that she had made a mistake by calling him while she was in bed. The deep timbre of his voice brushed across her skin like a velvet caress. The empty side of the bed where he slept seemed to mock her.

She fought to keep her mind off her husband and on their daughter. "She's in a fight mode now."

He chuckled. "Look out, Reese."

Unconsciously Denise smiled into the phone. There had never been any stopping Christine when she wanted something. Her father was the same way. Christine was willful at times, Edward was simply determined.

"Is she going back home?"

"No, she's staying here for a while." That was part of the plan. Christine had to show Reese that she didn't need him. Men wanted what they couldn't have, but Denise didn't think it prudent to bring that up.

Edward sighed. "As much as I hate hearing that, part of me is glad. I don't like you staying there alone."

She didn't like it either. She glanced again at the empty side of the bed, then at the picture window. This year, unlike every year since they'd moved into the house, there wasn't a live Christmas tree filled with twinkling white lights in front of it. But if things went as planned, there might be a tree yet. Then they could snuggle in bed, enjoying the lights and each other. It couldn't be too soon.

She missed the warmth of his body when she crawled between the cold sheets, the comfort of his arms, the steady beat of his heart beneath her cheek. She closed her eyes as longing swept through her.

"Dee, I think we should put up the lights. I saw Mr. Long the other day and he asked why they weren't up."

She sprang upright. Mr. Long was a kind old man, but his wife was the worst gossip in the city— scratch "city," make that the state. "What did you tell him?"

"That I'd been busy with work."

She made an instant decision. "You come by to-morrow. I'll have them out of the attic."

"You leave those heavy boxes alone," he ordered. "I'll get them."

"Edward, I'm not helpless."

"I never said you were."

Since that was so far from the truth she didn't dignify it with a response. "I just called so you wouldn't worry. Good night."

There was a long silence, and then, "I haven't had a good day or night since you asked for a divorce. I want you back in my life and us in our bed together," he told her tightly. "I'm going to keep reminding you of what we had until you remember."

"That's just it, Edward, I remember too much." Quietly she hung up the phone.

Sixteen

Lying on his back, Edward hung up the phone and stared at the ceiling. He tucked his hands beneath his head. Yes, he remembered too. Those early years of their marriage had been a challenge. They were both young, full of energy, and madly in love with each other.

He'd never forget the night Denise told him that she was pregnant with Christine. It was a moment of pure joy and sheer terror.

They were in bed in their small, one-bedroom apartment on the outskirts of Atlanta. It was a hot August night with hardly a breeze to be had. The white sheer curtains that Denise had made for their bedroom windows barely fluttered. He only wore a pair of briefs and Denise had on a short, hot pink nightgown that showed off her fabulous legs and did wonderful things for her chestnut complexion. She curled up next to him and stroked his chest, the scent of her freshly bathed and oiled body almost edible.

"Ed," she whispered.

"Hmmm?" He kissed the top of her head, brushing aside her short curls.

"I was thinking that maybe we should start looking for a bigger place."

"A bigger place?" He turned on his side to face her. "We really can't afford a bigger place now, Dee. Not with me still in school. This one is fine for the two of us. Just hang on, babe. I promise one day you'll have the biggest, fanciest house in the neighborhood."

"But . . . what if it was more than two of us?"

He sat up and looked down into her eyes, which seemed to sparkle in the moonlight. "What . . . are you saying?"

"Well . . . in about seven months there will be three of us."

"Dee . . ." His heart raced and it seemed that the room temperature had gone up at least another ten degrees. "Are you saying . . . ?"

She nodded. "I'm pregnant."

The world seemed to come to a standstill. For a moment, he couldn't think, couldn't breathe. How was he going to take care of a wife and child as a full-time student working two part-time jobs?

"Ed . . ."

He blinked and her face came back into focus.

"I know we said we'd wait. I know this means a big change in plans, but I can get a real job and help out with the bills and . . ."

He sat straight up. "Forget it. I promised you when we got married that I would take care of you. I mean that. If I have to work three jobs, that's what I'll do. I didn't want you working before and I certainly won't have my pregnant wife working now."

"But I want to help, Ed. This is my responsibility too."

"It's not up for debate, Denise. It's a man's responsibility to take care of his family and that's what I intend to do." He saw the disappointment in her eyes, but on this he had to be firm. He still had flashes of his mother coming home from work too tired to even look at him. He could still hear the arguments that his parents had about bills, the lack of food, heat, and decent clothes. He refused to do that to his wife and especially to his child. *My child.* He was going to be a father! And whatever it took, he was going to be the best father he possibly could.

"It's settled, Dee," he said. "I'm going to quit school and get a full-time gig. I'm sure Uncle Eddie can get me on one of the construction teams. It pays good money and I have some experience."

"You can't drop out of school! Ed, please . . ."

"What choice do I have, Dee? I'm not going to have you and my child want for anything. There's always time to go back . . . someday."

Denise lowered her head and he soon felt her tears on his bare chest. He gathered her close and stroked her back. "It's going to be okay, baby. I'll see to that. Don't you worry about a thing."

Have I been a thick-headed fool that long? he mused, as the memories receded. Even back then she'd been asking—no, telling him—she wanted to be a part of the marriage. But in his macho mind, he wouldn't hear of it. What an idiot!

So he'd dropped out of school, signed on with his uncle, and eventually he did go back to school at night to master his trade in design and construction. And the more the money started rolling in, the easier it became for him to have the final say-so in everything, from where they lived, the kind of cars they drove, the schools the children attended. Everything. Little by little, like water beating on a rock, he wore away the fabric of his marriage.

"Oh, Dee," he said aloud. "I'm so sorry, baby. I'm gonna make it all up to you, I swear I will."

"Lights out in there, Edward! I know I didn't hear you talking on the phone this time of night," Aunt Etta yelled from the other side of his door before shuffling down the hall.

He groaned. Making it up to Denise couldn't happen fast enough.

Morning arrived and Edward was ready to take the day by storm. After a brief meeting with the construction staff, he took a few moments to talk with William.

"I've located just about everything we need. As long as your dimensions are correct we should have enough material, with some to spare."

"Great. Well, I'm going to do a drive-by and see what's happening on the home front."

William chuckled. "No wonder you're looking so spiffy today. Not your usual work outfit."

Edward took a look at himself in the mirror. He'd purchased a new pair of black slacks and a lightweight burgundy turtleneck that showed off his abs. "If you're going to go a-courting, you have to go in style."

"I hear ya. Well, good luck. Think you might need me tonight?"

"Stay by the phone just in case. But I think I can handle some of it myself. And I have Anthony on call."

"Aye aye, Captain," he said, saluting.

Edward chuckled as William lock-stepped out of the office, then he pressed the intercom for Lena.

"Yes, Mr. Morrison?"

"I'm going over to the construction site and I won't be back for the rest of the day. If anything comes up, give me a call on my cell."

"Sure thing, Mr. Morrison."

Edward made a quick pit stop to check on the progress of the site, then headed downtown to the mall. He'd seen the perfect gift for Denise and he wanted to get it and stash it away. He stood in line for a good half hour to have the present gift wrapped and when he saw the exquisite finished product, he knew it was time well spent. After a few more stops to pick up some supplies, he darted to his temporary home to drop off Denise's gift and ran smack into Aunt Etta.

"Whatcha got there, son?" she asked, cornering him in the kitchen.

"It's my gift for Denise."

"Hope it's something romantic and not a vacuum cleaner." She laughed at her own joke.

"It's not a vacuum cleaner, Aunt Etta." He tried to get to his room.

Etta put her hand on his shoulder. "Sit down a minute, son."

He took a seat at the butcher block table.

"I want to tell you something you probably don't know anything about. It's about your dad."

"My father? What about him?" His brow creased in a frown.

"I know you got it in your head that your dad walked out on you and your mom. That he wasn't man enough to stick it out through the hard times." She lowered her head, then looked into his eyes. "It took a lot of courage to do what he did, Edward. Back in those days, if there was a man in the house Social Services wouldn't help you. Your dad knew that and so did your mother. They decided *together* what was best. It broke both of their hearts. And your father stayed away because he couldn't bear to see you and your mother and not be a part of your lives."

Edward's eyes filled as a knot formed in his throat.

"The things your father taught you about being a man, taking responsibility, sometimes it means letting go of the reins, son. Understand what I'm saying to ya?" She reached out and touched his cheek as a tear ran over her thumb.

"Why didn't anyone ever tell me?" he asked, his voice choked with emotion.

"We should have. Maybe you wouldn't have made some of the decisions that you did in your own life. Me and your uncle tried to do the best we could by you, son."

"I know. And I appreciate it. I really do."

"And you may think that your uncle is an old fool and that I just run all over him. Humph . . . as crazy as he is, I don't know what I would do without him. He makes me feel like I'm the most beautiful, the most important thing in his life. And I try to do the same, even if I have to knock him upside the head every now and then." She chuckled lightly, which brought a half smile to Edward's face. "You do the same for Denise, you hear me, son?"

"Yes, ma'am."

"She's giving you a hard time now and rightly so. This is your knot upside the head. Hope she knocks some sense into you before it's too late."

"I think she has, Aunt Etta. I think she has."

Seventeen

The sights and sounds of Christmas were everywhere. "White Christmas" played over the loudspeaker in the fabric store. The clerks all wore Santa hats. Holly looped around the checkout counter. People, who a month ago would cut you off to get to the cutting table first, were now full of the holiday spirit and insisted you go ahead of them. Denise had never felt less like joining in the festivities as she stood in line to have the fabric for Christine's dress cut.

Pushing the aching emptiness aside, she moved up in line. What was her next step in getting Edward to accept her independence and put the zip back in her marriage? She could guide him, but he had to get it on his own.

"You're making a party dress?"

Denise turned around to a smiling, middle-aged woman behind her. In her basket were a bolt of sheer red fabric, fringes, and tassels. "Yes, my daughter and her husband are going to a Christmas party this weekend. Is that what you're making?"

The well-dressed woman blushed, then glanced around and whispered, "My belly dancing costume."

Denise knew her mouth had fallen open and snapped it shut.

The woman laughed. "That's the same reaction my girlfriend had, but I read it's good exercise." She looked down at her round middle. "I certainly need it. Plus it's part of my husband's Christmas present."

Denise watched the twinkle in the other woman's eye and laughed. "I can tell he's going to be very pleased."

"Yes, he will, but then, so will I," she said with a wide grin.

"Next," called the harried clerk at the cutting table.

Placing the black jersey knit on the table, Denise told her how much she wanted, then impulsively turned back to the woman. "Would you happen to know if they have any more openings for the class?"

"I think so. Classes start Monday." The other woman dug in her small purse and pulled out a card. "Hope it works out."

"Thanks." Denise accepted the card, picked up the material, and headed for the checkout counter. *All right, Edward, time to get down.*

• • •

Afraid the class might fill up, Denise had called immediately after reaching her car. When she was informed there was one opening left, she drove to the dance studio and signed up. She had practically skipped back to her car. Edward would have a conniption. She grinned all the way back to the fabric store. After purchasing the things she needed, she had driven to Christine's office to show her. They'd laughed and giggled like schoolgirls.

Her good mood continued as she put on a pot of beef stew for dinner, then went to the attic to work on Christine's dress. They had settled on a design the night before. Her daughter had been almost as excited as when they'd worked on the sketches for her wedding gown.

Denise finished cutting out the dress, then frowned. The provocative creation only faintly resembled her original idea. While her own costume would be sheer, no one but the other females in the class and her instructor would see her. Christine's situation was different. Denise had wanted the long jersey dress to be backless with a high neck. Christine wanted it backless *and* cut artfully in front to show a bit of cleavage and stop just above her tiny waist. Denise hadn't been so sure about the idea.

"If I'm going to make his eyes pop, I might as well make them roll on the floor."

"Your father would have a fit," Denise had said while they were sitting on Christine's old bed, working on the sketch.

Her daughter had looked her in the eyes and said, "Daddy isn't doing this. We are."

Denise hadn't tried to dissuade her anymore. They were a team and she wasn't going to let Christine down. The party was tomorrow night and by the time Christine came home from work, she'd have finished hemming the gown and Christine could have her final fitting. Denise could start on her own costume tomorrow. Classes started Monday.

The day passed quickly as Denise worked on the dress and kept an eye on the stew. Finished except for the hem, she slipped the gown over the mannequin. She had to admit it suited Christine's passionate personality.

"Now for the decorations." Dismissing Edward's instructions, she started dragging out the boxes. There were lawn decorations of Santa and his reindeer racing into the sky after dropping off a load of brightly lit gifts beneath a twelve-foot Christmas tree that Edward had specially made. Then there were the hundreds of feet of twinkling white lights that would follow the pitch of the roof. As she reached for another box, she realized that her family wasn't the only one who enjoyed Christmas and all its magic and joy. So did she.

With the upheaval in her life, she needed to believe miracles still happened.

"I thought I'd find you up here."

Startled, Denise whirled at the sound of Edward's voice, almost falling backward. He easily caught her, pulling her up in front of him. His easy strength had always pleased and fascinated her. "What are you doing here? It's only a little after four."

"Saving you from a wrenched back," he told her. "You've gotten stubborn on me."

"Independent," she corrected.

He shook his head in exasperation, but a slow smile curved his mouth, unerringly drawing her gaze. She became aware of how close he was to her, aware of how much she missed him, and aware how much she hated sleeping alone.

His fingers tightened. "You still care."

"I never said I didn't," she admitted a bit breathlessly.

Passion flared in his dark eyes. He leaned down until his warm breath caressed her lips. "We're going to talk before the day is over. If two of my men weren't waiting outside, we'd do it now and a lot of other things I've been thinking about."

Denise felt her body tighten, but she had to make one thing clear. "Things *can't* be the way they were."

His mouth flattened into a hard line. "We had a good marriage."

"It was good for you," she said with asperity.

A shadow crossed his face. Misery stared back at her. "I thought you were happy."

If he hadn't looked so lost, so hurt, she would have brained him. "A happy woman doesn't ask for a divorce."

Calloused hands flexed on her arms. "You were happy once. I know it. What if I could make you happy again?"

Hope spiraled through her. "You can try."

"I'll do more than try. I'm coming after you." Whirling, he left, every bit of the self-assured man she had fallen in love with and married.

"Oh, my," Denise breathed. She could hardly wait.

Denise's day became even better later that evening on seeing the wide grin on Anthony's face when he greeted her at the front door.

"Hi, Mama. Reporting for duty. Did you remember to bake tea cakes?" he asked, picking up a box of decorations.

She laughed and pulled a palm-size, golden brown cookie from behind her back. Another tradition. "Fresh out of the oven."

Leaning over, he took a sizable bite from the cookie, then chewed with relish. "More."

"Wait your turn." Edward, who'd been standing to the side with a box of decorations in his hands, leaned over and bit into the cookie, the tip of his tongue touching Denise's hand.

She gasped. Her eyes widened as tremors radiated through her body.

Edward's eyes narrowed as he slowly chewed. "Some things get better with time."

Denise's heart thudded. "C-Christine should be here shortly and we can eat."

"Great. I'm starved." Anthony propped the box on his hip and reached for the remainder of the cookie with his free hand. "My turn, Dad." Munching, he went outside.

Denise's throat felt dry as she stared at Edward and he at her. "He's waiting."

"How about dinner Saturday night?" Edward asked. "Any place you choose."

"I have plans."

"Doing what?"

Denise raised her eyebrow at his brusque tone. She wasn't about to tell him she planned on being at home in case things didn't go as planned for Christine. "That's not your concern."

Setting the box down, he stepped closer until he

towered over her. "There was a time when I could change your mind."

Heat shimmered through her. Edward had coaxed and teased her out of her shyness during their courtship and marriage, teaching her to take her pleasure from him and give it in return. "You can't persuade me with sex," she told him softly.

"We never had sex. We had love, and it's still there." He leaned closer until she saw her own wide-eyed reflection in his deep brown eyes. "I see your pulse hammering in your throat, Dee. You want me as much as I want you."

"Intimacy was never our problem."

"You got that right." His hand touched her cheek before she could evade it, then he just as quickly turned, picked up the box, and sauntered out of the house after his son.

"Denise, this is great stew," Edward said, polishing off his second bowl. "Why aren't you eating?"

Because you keep looking at me like you used to when the children were younger and we couldn't wait to put them to bed so we could make love, she thought in rising irritation as she sat across from him. Who would have thought Edward could be devious?

"There's something about your cooking I always

enjoyed. Maybe it's just knowing you cooked it." He laughed. "You remember the spaghetti you cooked for me when we were dating?"

She scrunched up her face as the memory came to her. Edward hadn't had the money to take her out, so she'd invited him to dinner instead. Her grandmother had been at Wednesday night prayer service and Denise had been on her own.

She'd overcooked the spaghetti, burned the meat sauce and the garlic bread. Edward had eaten it anyway and ended up with indigestion. She'd been so embarrassed and felt so bad she had refused to see him when he came over a couple of days later.

"Hard to imagine Mama not being able to cook," Anthony said, polishing off another tea cake. "If there are any left I'm taking the rest home."

"I beg to differ." Christine shot an annoyed glance at her brother.

Unrepentant, Anthony grinned. "There's probably one or two left."

"If there isn't, you'll pay." Christine's eyes narrowed.

"You and what army?"

"I can still take you."

"Don't make me laugh."

"That's enough or I'll take all the remaining tea cakes for myself." Edward grinned at the stunned look on the children's faces. "If you two are finished, we can help your mother wash the dishes and clean up the kitchen."

Denise leisurely sipped her iced tea. Edward was definitely making progress.

Edward picked up his plate and hers. "You sit there and relax, Dee. The kids and I have it."

"Thank you." She could get used to being waited on.

"I was going back out to finish the lights," Anthony said.

"I want to try on my dress," was Christine's excuse.

At the sink, Edward turned. "Then the sooner we finish, the quicker you two can do what you want. Afterward I thought we'd go down to the tree lot and get a Christmas tree."

Denise opened her mouth to disagree, but the children bounded up, their faces shining. Another family tradition. This year it was Christine's turn to put the angel on top.

Denise sipped her tea and watched the unusual sight of her husband washing dishes. Time would tell if this change was permanent or if he was simply going through the motions. She knew one thing. This round went to him.

"No daughter of mine is wearing a dress like that," Edward railed, his hands on his lean hips as he stared at Christine in her party dress.

"I certainly wouldn't let Sherri go out in a dress like that." Anthony folded his arms across his chest. "Looks like that dress J.Lo wore at the Oscars."

In the middle of the family room, Christine's chin lifted a fraction. A sure sign that she was ready to fight. "I love you, Daddy, but I'm wearing this dress. It's just what I wanted."

"Denise."

"Mama."

All eyes converged on her. In Edward's face she saw disapproval and demand for her to follow his lead, just as she always had. In Christine's was a plea for help to fight for her husband. Unconsciously, Denise's chin lifted in an exact imitation of her daughter. "It's daring and provocative, but not risqué or vulgar. I think she looks stunning."

Christine squealed and ran across the room to grab her mother. "Thank you. Thank you. This will certainly make Reese take notice."

Edward's eyes narrowed with disapproval. "Is this how you're helping her?"

Denise felt Christine tense beside her. They'd never argued in front of the children, or anywhere else for that matter, because Denise always gave in. "Reese needs a wake-up call before it's too late."

"Wake up to what?" Edward asked.

"To realize that he has a beautiful, desirable wife

and he had better pay attention to her before some-one else does."

Edward's expression hardened. He stalked over to her. "Is that what this is about?"

"I'm going up to change." Christine headed for the stairs, dragging Anthony with her.

Denise didn't shrink from her husband's anger. She knew if she did, she might as well give up and give in. "I was talking about Reese and Christine. Not us."

"You don't think I pay attention to you, do you?" he asked, apparently not convinced.

Lying didn't enter her mind. "No, you don't."

Edward opened his mouth, then closed it and took a deep breath in an apparent attempt to calm down. "I do."

"If you can answer one simple question, I'll apologize."

"And call off the divorce procedures?" Edward quickly asked.

Denise hesitated. "Yes, but if I'm right, you sign the papers to sell the house."

The pleased smile on his face disappeared. "That isn't fair."

Denise shrugged carelessly, although she knew the outcome. Edward needed another wake-up call. "You said you pay attention to me. What's the risk?

I'll answer the same question about you or any other question you ask."

Edward stared at her and rubbed the back of his neck as if trying to figure out if she planned to trick him. "Oh, all right. What's the question?"

"What was I wearing and what color was it the last time we saw each other?"

His eyes narrowed. Clearly he hadn't expected the question. His gaze flickered over her red cardigan and jeans. "That's an easy question for you. I always wear jeans."

"But you had on a chambray shirt," she said calmly. "What did I have on? Forget about the color."

He moistened his lips "A sweater and pants."

Her smile was sad. "A white blouse and black skirt."

"Dee."

She stepped back from his reaching hands. "I'll get the papers. Afterward we can go get the tree." Quietly, she walked from the room.

If this new development didn't keep him on his toes and hustling to win her back, seeing her in her belly dancing costume certainly would.

Eighteen

Edward watched in disbelief as Denise climbed the stairs and entered what was once *their* bedroom, shutting the door solidly behind her. He'd really blown it this time. Was he that out of tune to his wife? Did he really not "see" her and only took her presence for granted? No wonder she wanted out. He took a last look up the steps before heading out. "All of that is going to change, babe. I guarantee it. You're turning into a new woman and you're going to have a new man."

He opened the front door and stepped outside. He needed some air. The minute he crossed the threshold his cell phone rang. Checking the number, he saw that it was William. Damn, he'd forgotten all about calling him.

"Yeah, man. What's up?" Edward asked, closing the door behind him.

"How'd it go?" William asked. "I was waiting for

your call. Will you be able to get her out of the house for a couple of hours tonight, or what?"

Edward frowned, faced now with the new ultimatum from Denise. "I don't know, man, but I'll dial you back if the coast is clear and it's not too late."

"You don't sound good. Did something else happen?"

Edward walked over to his SUV and got in. He was pensive for a moment before finally confiding in his friend. He started in the middle.

"I don't know, man. I guess I have been living in my own world for so long that I really haven't been paying attention to anything or anyone. I've been under the notion that as long as the bills were paid, there was food in the fridge, and everyone was healthy, that it was all good."

"But that's what a man is expected to do," William said, using the remote to change the channels on his television. "I think you're being too hard on yourself."

"Yeah, but at the same time a man can't be so blind and deaf that he can't see or hear what's truly happening in his own house."

"What happened? When you left this afternoon you were so positive and upbeat." He settled on an Atlanta Hawks basketball game. "Did you two have a fight or something?"

Edward shook his head and chuckled derisively. "I wish it was that simple."

"Then what happened?" William picked up a bottle of beer and took a long swig.

"Denise asked me a simple question. What was she wearing and what color it was the last time we saw each other."

"Oh, naw, man, don't tell me you went for that one? It's the oldest female trick in the book." He laughed and shook his head. "That's the equivalent of 'Do I look too fat in this outfit?'" He put down the beer and took a handful of chips, chewing as he spoke. "They will get you every time with that one. Or, 'Do you like this dress better than this one on me?' No matter what answer you give, it will be the wrong one."

Edward had to laugh. "Yeah, I see what you mean. So, do you think when Denise said that if I gave the wrong answer I would agree to sign the papers to sell the house that she was just pulling my leg?" he asked, his tone serious.

"Whoa. That's what she did?"

Edward nodded.

"Hmmm. To be truthful, Ed, I really think that Denise just wants you to pay her attention. I mean, really pay her attention. In all the years I've known you two she never seemed to want out, never seemed not to truly love you and the kids. I mean, have to admit, I'm no whiz when it comes to figuring out the complex minds of women, but on this one I would have to say she's trying to put the screws to you, my brother."

"Well, she's doing a damned good job of it. The thing is, the more I'm around her the less I seem to know her. She's a completely different woman. In all of our twenty-seven years of marriage, Dee has always been quiet, unimpulsive, loving, and dependable. Now when I drop by, there's no telling what or *who* I'm going to find."

"That's the joy of married life," he said with a chuckle. "What did Forrest Gump say in the movie? 'Life is like a box of chocolates, you never know what you're going to get.' Hey, that's what marriage is, a box of chocolates."

"They also say diamonds are a girl's best friend, but chocolate can go a long way too."

"Huh?"

"I'll call you later. I have to make a quick run."

"Okay, I'll be waiting. Leslie is at her mother's house for the weekend so I have plenty of time."

Who knew what Denise would think when she came back downstairs and found me gone? Edward mused as he zipped down the street into the center of town. It was a little after six, but with the holidays right around the corner the shops stayed open as late as possible trying to entice shoppers.

He cruised around for a few minutes until he found a parking space not far from the Chocolate Factory. When he stepped inside he was blown away to find the shop overflowing with men! He shook his head, wondering how many of them were in the same precarious situation as he.

After a good twenty minutes of waiting, it was finally Edward's turn on line.

"May I help you, sir?" the cheery salesclerk, dressed in a Ms. Claus outfit, asked. "Something for Christmas for your wife?" she asked, spotting his gold wedding band.

"Something pre-Christmas, actually," Edward murmured, fumbling for the right words.

The salesclerk looked at him curiously. "A makeup gift?" she whispered.

"Hmmm, more like a courting gift."

"I see." She smiled in understanding. "Do you have a price range in mind?"

"Price is no object," he said, tapping the wallet filled with credit cards in his back pocket.

"Well, let me show you what we have."

More than a half hour later, loaded down with a bright red shopping bag tied with pink ribbon, Edward headed back home.

· · · ·

When Denise returned back downstairs with the papers of sale in hand, Edward was nowhere to be found. She peeked out the window and saw that his SUV was gone as well. She started to go back upstairs and ask her children if their father said anything before disappearing, but changed her mind. The last thing she needed was for them to think things were even worse than they already were.

She dropped the curtain back in place. Had she pushed her hand too hard? Her goal had not been to run him away, but to bring him back into her arms— totally. Edward had never been a man who could easily be manipulated. He was single-minded and determined. His home and family were important to him and she'd threatened that.

Denise took a seat on the couch, her heart heavy and her thoughts in disarray. But on the other hand, Edward was not a man to give up easily either, she reasoned. He'd made it clear earlier in the day that his intention was to win her back. For a moment her hopes were renewed, but just as quickly reality hit. Edward was gone. Gone. Gone after she'd told him he'd blown it for the last time. She told him he would sign the papers to sell the house, the last step in severing their relationship.

She covered her face with her hands to hold back a sob, just as the doorbell rang. Blinking back tears, she pulled herself together and went to the door, figuring it was her nosy neighbor wondering when they were going to finish putting up their lights. She pulled the door open to find the last person she expected to see.

"Paul! I mean, Mr. Carter. What are you doing here?" She looked past him, praying that Edward really wasn't in the vicinity.

"Good evening, Mrs. Morrison. Sorry to just drop by unannounced. But I've tried to reach Christine and can't get ahold of her. I wanted to give her a small Christmas gift."

Denise's brows rose in surprise. "Oh, I see. Well . . . Christine is upstairs." She took another peek around him. "I can get her for you, if you want to wait a minute."

"That would be great, if it's not a problem."

She stepped back and let him pass. "Have a seat in the living room and I'll get her."

"Thanks."

He walked inside and Denise darted upstairs. She found Christine and Anthony sitting on the floor of his room listening to music.

"Uh, Christine, can I see you for a minute?"

Christine pulled herself up from the floor. "Sure, Mom."

The instant Christine was at the door, Denise snatched her by the arm and pulled her into the hall.

"You'll never guess who's downstairs," she said in an urgent whisper, her eyes wide with alarm.

"Who?" Christine hissed back.

"Paul Carter."

"What!"

"Yes, and he said he came to see *you*. He even brought a gift."

"What!"

"Are you having trouble hearing me? I'm telling you that man is downstairs bearing gifts for you! What in heaven's name did you tell him?"

Christine frowned. "I . . . I didn't tell him anything, other than I needed his help with my mom and dad and if he would mind just playing along. I didn't go into detail, if that's what you mean."

Denise rolled her eyes to the heavens. "Well, he must have read your signals wrong. Why else would he just turn up? He said he'd been trying to reach you."

Christine squeezed up her face. "Maybe I did kind of lay it on thick," she sheepishly admitted.

"Well, you better get down there and remove a few layers. We have enough to contend with at the moment."

"Where's Daddy?" she asked, heading downstairs.

"I have no idea. When I went back down he was gone. And the last person I want him to see, if he decides to come back, is Paul Carter. He nearly had a seizure the first time." She giggled, remembering the thunder and lightning expression on Edward's face. "Go on, go on," Denise urged.

"All right, all right. But what am I going to say?"

"Just graciously accept the gift, tell him 'No, you shouldn't have,' and send him on his merry way." Denise bit down on her fingernail, imagining all the possible scenarios if Edward walked through the door. "Hurry up," she insisted.

"I'm going. Just wait right here."

Christine headed downstairs while Denise practically hung over the banister trying to overhear the conversation.

"What's going on?" Anthony asked, coming up behind her.

Denise almost leaped over the railing, "Boy! Don't you know it's not polite to sneak up on people?" she squeaked, turning to her son.

"Jeez, I just asked a question. You don't have to bite my head off." He peered over the railing. "Who's Christine talking to anyway? I thought I heard the bell."

"Uh . . . just a friend who stopped by to say hello."

"Really? Who?" He started for the stairs.

Denise grabbed his arm just as the bell rang again. She let out a gasp.

"Mom! What's wrong with you?"

"Nothing. Go to your room."

"What?"

"I mean, why don't you go on back in your room and I'll get the door?" She forced a smile.

The bell rang again.

Before Denise could get to the door, Christine answered it.

"Reese! What are you doing here?"

"I wanted to see you." He slung his hands in his pants pockets. "Can I come in?"

"Uh . . ."

"Reese, what a surprise," Denise said, stepping up beside Christine. She slid her arm around her daughter's waist.

They both stood in the doorway like sentinels, just as Edward's SUV pulled up in the driveway.

Denise groaned.

Christine turned to her mother, her eyes wide with alarm, asking the silent question, *What do we do now?*

"Reese, this is a surprise," Edward said, mounting the steps to the front door. "Are you coming or going?"

"I thought I'd stop by and see Chris, but . . ."

"But what?" He looked at the frozen expressions of his wife and daughter.

"Hey, Dad, Reese," Anthony said, joining the posse at the door.

"Can we come in or are you going to make us stand here?" Edward asked, brushing by Denise and Christine with Reese on his heels.

Both men came to a complete halt when they saw Paul sitting on the love seat in the living room with Denise, Christine, and Anthony nearly falling over one another when the parade came to a stop.

Paul stood, his ever-ready smile in place. "Mr. Morrison." He stuck out his hand, which Edward reluctantly shook. "Happy holidays. Good to see you again."

Edward grunted something unintelligible.

He turned toward Anthony. "Paul Carter," he said by way of introduction.

"Anthony Morrison, Christine's brother," he said with a smile, oblivious to the tension in the room.

"Yes, Christine mentioned she had a brother." He shook Anthony's hand, then turned to Reese.

"Reese Evans, Christine's husband," he said, enunciating every word.

"Christine has told me all about you. Glad to finally meet you."

"Funny, Christine never mentioned you."

"Oh," he said and chuckled lightly. "Christine and I are old college friends. I stopped by to drop off a thank-you gift to the Morrisons."

"Thank-you gift?" Edward asked.

Denise and Christine shared a look of terror.

"Yes, I was working on selling the house for them. I generally pick up a token of thanks for all my potential clients during the holidays," he said as smooth as a good shot of brandy. "Well, this is obviously a family night and I won't intrude any further." He started for the door. "Enjoy your holidays, folks."

Christine and Denise followed him to the door. He turned to face them.

"Thank you," they whispered in unison.

"No problem. I hope everything works out . . . for both of you." He handed the brightly wrapped gift to Denise. "Might as well make it look good," he said. He looked at Christine and smiled. "Ask your mom to share those with you." He winked and walked away.

Sighing deeply, Denise and Christine turned in unison and faced the questioning faces of the men in their lives.

"Well," Denise said, full of forced cheer, "a night of surprises." She smiled brightly. "We have our first gift." She marched over to the mantel and set the square box next to their wedding picture.

Christine straightened her shoulders and tilted up her chin. "You wanted to talk to me, Reese," she stated more than asked and plopped down on the couch, folding her arms beneath her breasts.

Reese cleared his throat, looking uncomfortable for a minute. "Yes, about the party tomorrow night."

"I'll get working on the lights," Anthony said, finally getting his cue.

Edward stepped up to Denise at the mantel and cupped her upper arm. "I think you and I need to talk too," he said in a low rumble, hustling her out of the room and out the front door before she could utter a word of protest.

Once outside, he opened the door of his SUV. "Get in."

Denise huffed but got inside. "Are we going somewhere?" she asked.

"That's what I want to know. Are we, Dee?"

"It's entirely up to you, Edward," she said, holding her ground.

"If it were entirely up to me, we wouldn't be having this conversation in the first place."

"I see."

"Do you?" he said, his voice dropping to a throbbing low tone.

She turned to look at him and her heart knocked hard in her chest. He was so close, close enough to . . .

He reached over into the backseat and pulled up

the red shopping bag. "I got something for you."

"Edward, you didn't have to buy me something," she murmured, taking the bag and holding it to her chest.

"I know I didn't. I wanted to." His smile was gentle. "I want things to be the way they were, Dee. Well, maybe not exactly, but . . ." He took a breath. "I'm not signing any papers. I just want you to know that. You're going to have to make me truly believe that you don't love me, that I can't make it up to you, and that you don't want to live with me anymore. Until you do that, I'm going to make it hard as hell for you to walk away from me." He turned the key in the ignition. "Now, let's go get that tree."

He pulled off into the twilight, and Denise wondered how much longer she could hold out.

Several hours later, the tree was up, the house was lit, and the ragtag family stood around admiring their handiwork.

Anthony yawned. "Well, folks, I think I'll be heading home." He stood and stretched, said his good-byes, and headed out.

"Me too," Reese said shortly, after looking longingly at his wife.

Christine swallowed hard. "I guess I'll see you

tomorrow . . . for the party. That is, if you still want to go."

"I'll be here," he said quietly. He picked up his jacket from the back of the couch and slipped it on. "Can you walk me to the door, Chris?"

Christine got up from the floor and followed him out.

"Chris, I don't like this. I miss you. I'm sorry about everything. I want you to come home." He took her hand in his.

"I still need some time to think, Reese," she said. "I have to learn to trust you all over again."

"You will. I promise." He leaned forward and kissed her cheek. "See you tomorrow."

"Good night, Reese."

She watched him get into his car and couldn't wait until tomorrow night when he saw her in her dress. The days and nights of being without him would be well worth it when she saw the look in his eyes. She closed the door, smiled, and practically skipped upstairs, waving good night to her family on the way.

"Guess that just leaves me and you," Edward said with a sparkle in his eyes as he eased closer to Denise on the couch. "The kids are gone, the house is quiet . . ." He leaned over and kissed her gently on the ear.

A shiver like an electric shock raced through her. "Ed . . ."

"What?" he whispered, his warm breath running along her neck. He traced the shell of her ear with his fingertip.

She closed her eyes, relishing in the sensation of his touch and then suddenly, as if cold water had been tossed on her, he jumped up.

"Gee, look at the time," he said, checking his watch and then shrugging into his jacket. He looked down at her and smiled that boyish smile of his. "Gotta be going." He put on his baseball cap and tugged it down over his brow.

It took all the control she could muster not to scream.

She let out a breath and returned his smile. "Yes, it is getting late," she said from between clenched teeth.

"Maybe I'll see you tomorrow. If not, I'll call." He walked to the door. "Rest well," he said and shut the door behind him.

Denise jumped up and stomped her foot in frustration. *So that's how he's going to play it*, she thought, her hormones raging. *Fine.*

She glanced across the room and saw the red shopping bag. Snatching it up, she took it to her room. Sitting on the big king-size bed, she debated about opening it before Christmas.

"He did say it was a pre-Christmas gift," she muttered, reaching for the box.

When she finally got past all the ribbon and wrapping and got the box open, she sat back and nearly cried.

Inside the box were two twelve-inch chocolate figures of a man and woman surrounded by an assortment of chocolate delights. But what stole her heart was the note tucked in the box.

> *Marriage is like savoring a box of chocolates . . . some moments will be sweet, others sticky, some will bring tears to your eyes, and others will make you see heaven. Each one is like a day with you, Denise, filled with surprises. Whatever it might hold, I want to discover it all with you.*
>
> *Love, Ed.*

"Oh Edward," she said, nearly weeping as she reached for one of the delicacies and popped it into her mouth.

She curled up on the bed with the box tucked beneath her arm. "Maybe you are getting it after all," she whispered, a smile blooming on her lips. "But just for assurance's sake, I still have a trick or two up my sleeve."

Nineteen

Reese sat perched on the edge of the living room sofa on Saturday night, his head bowed, his folded hands between his long legs. Denise watched the silent young man and waited for her daughter to come downstairs. She felt sorry for him, but he did need a wake-up call. "I'm glad you and Christine are going to the party together."

Slowly he raised his head. Misery stared back at her. "I didn't want her driving back by herself late at night, especially with all the heavy holiday traffic." He pushed his glasses back on the bridge of his nose. "I love Christine. I want you to know that. I'm not sure what's happening, but I just wanted you to know."

Denise sent him a warm, encouraging smile. "I'm sure you do, Reese, but Christine is the one you have to convince."

"Ready."

Reese jerked around at the sound of Christine's voice. His mouth gaped. Slowly he came to his feet. "Christine." There was awe in his voice as he stared at her standing in the doorway.

Denise glanced at Christine. She was stunning in the provocative gown.

"I'm ready to go," Christine said, then crossed to her mother and bent to kiss her on the cheek. "Thank you."

Denise briefly clasped her hand. "Have fun."

Christine's eyes twinkled. "I intend to." Straightening, she turned her back to Reese and held out the wrap for him to help her.

Reese's sharp intake of breath cut through the room. The backless gown barely skimmed the smooth brown curve of her back. "Christine!"

She glanced beguilingly over her shoulder. "Yes, Reese?"

He gulped. "Your—your dress."

"Beautiful, isn't it?" she replied. "Mama made it for me."

Reese's wide eyes swung to Denise. She smiled sweetly. He couldn't very well say anything bad about a gown her mother made, and certainly not while Denise was in the same room.

"If you've changed your mind, Reese, I can go by

myself. Since it's being given by the hospital, several of my friends will be there," Christine told him.

Denise smothered a laugh as Reese, moving faster than she'd ever seen, raced across the room and took the wrap from her hand. "No. You're going with me." He draped it around her smooth, bare shoulders, his hands lingering possessively.

"Thank you. We'd better get going."

He nodded absently. "All right."

"Good night, Mama."

"Good night," Denise said, coming to her feet and giving Christine a discreet thumbs-up. "Have fun."

"I certainly plan to. I can't wait to dance."

Reese's arm tightened. "Maybe you should just dance with me."

Christine batted her lush, long eyelashes. "But you don't like to dance."

"Tonight is an exception."

"We'll see," she said, stopping in front of the door and waiting for Reese to open it.

Denise's lips twitched. Christine was in a reckless mood.

Frowning, Reese opened the door. "We'll talk in the car."

"Talk about what?" asked a deep male voice.

"Daddy!" Christine greeted, going up on tiptoes to give him a hug.

Reese swallowed. "Good evening, Mr. Morrison."

Edward peered down from his six-inch advantage at his son-in-law. "Good to see you again, Reese."

The young man visibly relaxed. "Thank you, sir."

Edward stepped aside. "Don't let me keep you."

"Good night, Mr. Morrison. Mrs. Morrison." Taking Christine's arm, he guided her down to his late-model Lexus.

Denise waved as they drove off, then came inside. Edward followed. "I'm glad you got here in time to see Christine off. She did look beautiful in her gown."

"I saw that, but that's not why I'm here."

"Oh?" Denise tried to read his expression and couldn't.

"The first reason is to apologize for the way I went off about her dress. I called her today and told her. It was a knee-jerk reaction. I've always trusted you to make the right decisions for the children and you have."

Denise felt like pumping her fist. *Go, Edward!* "The second reason?"

"Guess?"

Butterflies took flight in her stomach at the intense way he was looking at her. Was he there to take up where they had left off last night? Would she let him?

"We're going to spend some time together where

I can pay attention to the woman I love." He grabbed her hand and pulled her back outside. "Let's go for a walk and look at the Christmas decorations."

She stared at him. "It's fifty degrees out here."

Shrugging off his suede jacket, he wrapped it around her shoulders, then grinned devilishly down at her. "Come on, I'll keep you warm just like I used to."

As always Edward tempted her, but she had too much to do to catch a cold. "I have things to do."

Ignoring her protests, he closed the front door. "They can wait. You have on a thick sweater and wool pants. I'm wearing a flannel shirt and jeans. So stop stalling."

"My body doesn't generate heat like a furnace the way yours does." She couldn't believe this. He wasn't the impulsive type. "I didn't get my key and I have nothing on my head."

"I have my key." He frowned down at her as if he'd like to shake her, then plopped his baseball cap on her head. "Now, will you stop complaining?"

Denise opened her mouth to say she wasn't complaining, then snapped it shut. "Are they showing re-runs of your favorite TV programs? On Saturday nights you wouldn't budge from that hideous chair from seven until you went to bed . . . unless it was to get food or a soft drink."

"Jeez." He slung his arm around her shoulder and started down the curved walkway. "This is what I get for listening to Uncle Eddie and Aunt Etta."

"Whoa." Denise stopped and stared incredulously up at Edward. "You're taking advice from your uncle and aunt?" she asked, laughing.

"They certainly know something I don't. They're at each other every night," he said with an equal amount of envy and admiration.

Denise choked. Edward's large hand pounding her back made it worse. "Stop," she coughed, then caught her breath enough to look at him. "You're serious?"

Grim-faced, he nodded. "They want me in bed every night by nine."

They looked at each other and started laughing so hard they had to hold each other up. The laughter ceased when Denise realized Edward's arms were around her waist, pressing her body firmly to his, his face inches from hers. She couldn't move, and when his mouth settled on hers, she ceased to think.

Hunger shot through her. She reached for him, her need as desperate as the arms locked around her. She missed the taste, the texture, the overpowering desire he ignited in her.

The sudden blast of a car horn tore them apart. Passing down the street in his twenty-year-old Cadillac was Mr. Long and his wife, who had her nose pressed to the car window.

"Spoilsports. We were enjoying the show."

Denise and Edward jerked around to see Jeff and Monique Patterson, the couple next door, standing midway of their walk and grinning from ear to ear. They'd moved in a few years ago and were expecting their first baby in January.

"W-we were going to look at the lights," Denise said.

"Yeah, right," Jeff said, hugging his wife as she elbowed him in the side.

"I think it's sweet," Monique said, leaning her heavy body against her husband's. "I hope we're as affectionate in the years to come."

Denise felt like a fraud. "You doing all right, Monique?"

She smiled. "The baby is practicing kicking field goals again." She was bundled up with a heavy wool coat that couldn't possibly reach around her protruding stomach, a scarf, and boots. "I thought walking might help."

"Why don't you join us?" Edward said, sliding his arm around Denise's shoulder. "I can give Jeff some pointers on changing diapers and making formula, and I don't think there's ever been a better mother than Denise."

Denise stared up at her husband, a pleasant warmth stealing into her heart. He was definitely doing and saying the right things tonight. She just might get her Christmas miracle.

They set off at an easy pace, with the Pattersons in front. Edward still had his arm around Denise's shoulder. She certainly wasn't going to complain. She had missed having him close to her.

Occasionally they'd stop to admire the glittering Christmas lights in a rainbow of colors or stark white on almost every house. Those that weren't decorated soon would be. Many homes had the new icicle lights, but a few still had the old rope lights. As they ambled down the street, people waved and asked the Pattersons about the impending birth of their baby. They had good neighbors. Their decision to raise their children here had been a sound one.

Seeing a nativity scene on the lawn at the end of the block, Monique stopped and placed her hands on top of her stomach. "It's beautiful. I can't wait to hold our baby in my arms."

Denise came up beside her and felt Edward's arms go around her waist. She was powerless to keep from leaning back against him. "You fall totally, hopelessly in love the moment you set eyes on your baby. I couldn't stop crying."

"I wasn't too dry-eyed myself," Edward admitted quietly, his chin resting on top of Denise's head.

"Yet I'd never been more scared in my life."

"Of what?" Jeff asked. "The worst part was over."

Edward's arms tightened. "It was just the beginning. I now had two people depending on me. I never wanted Denise or Christine or Anthony, who came later, to want for anything."

"We didn't," Denise admitted truthfully; Edward had held down two jobs to care for them. "We couldn't have asked for better."

"My father wasn't there for me when I got older," Edward said, his voice quiet in the night. "I swore I'd always be there for my family."

"That's just how I feel," Jeff said. "A man's got to take care of his family."

Out of the corner of her eye, Denise saw the almost imperceptible shake of Monique's head. So Jeff was another man who thought women's brains turned to mush when they married.

"But don't smother your wife and children or try to live their lives for them," Denise said to Jeff before she thought. "Love them, but give them room to grow, to make their own mistakes."

For a moment Jeff looked taken aback, then he grinned sheepishly. "You've been talking to Monique."

"No. I've been living with Edward for twenty-seven years." The younger couple laughed. Denise joined in. Only Edward was silent.

• • •

Edward remained quiet as they started back. After saying good night to the Pattersons, she invited him in for coffee, but he made no attempt to drink it. "Would you like a tea cake?"

He looked up from sitting at the island in the kitchen. "It wasn't my intention to smother you."

Without thought, she crossed the room and placed her hand on top of his. "You're a wonderful man even if you make me want to strangle you at times."

His other hand settled on hers. "What about the other times?"

"I felt as if I was the luckiest woman in the world," she admitted honestly, then stepped back when he reached for her. "But sometimes isn't enough."

"All or nothing, is that it?" he asked, a hint of challenge in his voice.

"Yes."

He finally picked up his coffee cup. "Is Christine coming back tonight?"

Denise wasn't sure how to take the change of subject. "I don't know."

He stared at her over the rim. "What was Reese's reaction to the dress?"

Relaxing, Denise smiled and picked up her own coffee. "He wasn't able to take his eyes off her."

"So, he's going through sensitivity training too."

Denise straightened, remembering why she never played card games with Edward. He'd lull you, and then . . . wham! "He's learning to appreciate her."

"Hmmm." Setting the cup aside, Edward came off the stool and didn't stop until his body was pressed against hers. She felt the hard delineation of his muscled body from her suddenly aching nipples to her quivering thighs.

"Edward," she said breathlessly. "W-what are you doing?"

His arms bracketed her, preventing her from moving. "I've been thinking about what you said about not making love in bed all the time."

"E-Edward."

His tongue grazed her lower lip, causing her to shiver. "I think you're right. I seem to remember one memorable occasion right where we're standing, while the kids were at the movies." He nuzzled her neck. "You came apart in my arms."

"*Edward.*"

"I'm here, Dee," he crooned. "I'll always be here."

Denise felt herself slipping under his spell. It had been so long and he felt so good.

The ring of his cell phone shattered the spell. Edward muttered an expletive.

Denise didn't know if she was thankful or annoyed. She did know she wasn't sure if her legs could support her if she tried to move.

Edward snatched the cell phone from his belt loop. "Yeah!"

"Don't you take that tone with me, boy," Denise heard Uncle Eddie yell. "It's past nine. If you're not home in fifteen minutes you'll be sleeping outside." The line went dead.

Edward's head fell forward. "There's not a jury in the world that would convict me."

Denise's lips twitched. "They love you."

"And I was about to get some good loving," he growled.

"That's what *you* think." Denise shoved him aside and headed for the front door. "Good night. I have things to do."

"Denise."

She turned and found herself in his arms. Her hands pressed against his broad chest. "You'll have to sleep outside," she warned.

"It will be worth it." His mouth pressed possessively against hers, taking, giving, sending heat and desire racing through her. Her body yielded. She felt herself being lowered and then the area rug beneath her. His mouth left hers to roam greedily over her face. Lights flickered. It took Denise a moment to realize they were lights from the Christmas tree.

They'd made love beneath the Christmas tree, too. But if they made love now, before things were completely settled between them, it would only complicate matters. He was doing and saying the right things, but she wasn't entirely convinced he'd continue if she called off the divorce. Could a man change twenty-seven years of behavior in a matter of weeks? She was betting he could if the love was strong enough. But in the meantime . . .

"Edward, stop."

His mouth hovered above hers. "You don't want me to."

"Yes, I do."

His eyes shut briefly, then he stood gracefully. "I want you back in my life and I'm not going to rest until you are."

Denise watched him leave, then came up on her knees in front of the twelve-foot pine decorated with twenty-seven years of memories and love. Directly in front of her was a handmade ornament she'd sewn of white satin and red thread that said *First Christmas*. Her finger traced the words. They'd been poor but so in love. She wanted that love for them again.

Leaning back on her heels, she looked at the beautiful black angel on top of the tree, with her wings outspread and open arms. "Please, let it be the real deal."

Twenty

Edward was up with the sun, having barely slept through the night as sexy visions of his wife kept him on simmer. It had taken all his home training to keep from ravishing her, but as he'd slowly come to realize, a good marriage needed more than just good loving. With it being Sunday morning, short of a natural disaster, Denise went to church—with or without him—where she spent the better part of the morning, followed by a late brunch with Christine. He grinned as the steamy water streamed over his body. Thank goodness for habits. But this would be a Sunday without him.

Drying quickly and donning a pair of jeans and a work shirt, he called Anthony and then William and told them both to meet him at the house in an hour. He'd already called Denise to ensure that she was gone. He had less than two weeks to pull this off, and it was one deadline he had no intention of missing.

• • •

By the time Edward arrived at the house, Anthony's Acura and William's Jeep were parked out front. They stepped out of their vehicles when Edward approached.

"Hey, guys. Thanks for coming."

"No problem," William said, shaking Edward's hand. "Let's do this."

Edward clapped Anthony on the back. "Thanks, son."

"Sure. But we should get busy. Mom usually gets home around three."

Edward checked his watch. "That gives us five hours."

"We can get plenty done in that time. Let me start unloading." He headed for his Escalade.

"I'll help," Anthony offered.

"Naw. I'm cool," he said, waving Anthony off. "You two can get started inside."

"Good idea. Come on, son."

"I'm glad you're doing this, Dad," Anthony said as they strolled down the driveway.

"Really? Why?" He looked at his son expectantly.

Anthony shrugged. "I think it will mean a lot to Mom."

"I hope so."

"Dad?"

"Hmmm?"

"Are you and Mom really getting divorced? I mean, the other night with the real estate guy . . . she seems serious. But then sometimes I see her looking at you when she doesn't think anyone is watching and . . . well, I don't know . . ." He looked at his father, hoping for answers.

"In my heart I have to believe it's not what she really wants."

"Then why?" he asked, truly perplexed.

Edward halted at the end of the driveway and turned to Anthony. "Your mother wants me to wake up and smell the coffee. She wants to put the fear of God in me."

"Has she?"

"You better believe it." He chuckled halfheart-edly. "To be honest, son, when your mother told me she wanted a divorce and wanted to sell the house, I've never been so scared in my entire life. It terri-fied me to think that I could lose everything I loved in one fell swoop." He shook his head. "I can't imagine my life without your mother."

"Have you told her that?"

Edward blinked and focused on his son. He put his hand on Anthony's shoulder. "It's not that sim-ple. It has to be more than words."

"Like what?" He frowned in confusion.

"I'm still trying to figure that out. But in the

meantime, this is a start. And I'll keep trying until I get it right."

"Hey guys, your Uncle Eddie just pulled up," William said, hauling supplies on a dolly.

"Uncle Eddie!" they cried in unison.

"And your aunt."

"Oh, no," Edward groaned.

"What are we going to do, Dad? You know Aunt Etta couldn't keep a secret even for a fifth of Jack Daniel's, and Uncle Eddie is worse."

Edward ran his hand across his face. "I'll take them in the house. You two get as much done as you can. I'll chat them up for a few and get them out of here as soon as possible."

"Okay."

Edward darted to the front of the house, just as Etta and Eddie alighted from their 1968 Cadillac Seville. The car was enormous and a gas guzzler. It sounded like all the screws were loose when it came down the street, but Eddie refused to get rid of it. "Just 'cause something is old and noisy doesn't mean you get rid of it," Eddie would say in defense of his car whenever someone suggested that he get a new one. "Etta's old and noisy. What if I traded her in for a new one?" To which Etta would promptly pop him in the head with whatever was available. "Ouch, woman!" And then it would be on. Oh, Lawd, he couldn't take those two today.

"Uncle Eddie, Aunt Etta," he greeted full of good cheer, catching them at the front door. "What are you two doing here?"

"We were coming home from early church service," Etta began, "which is someplace you needed to be this morning." Her eyes squeezed into two slits. "Need to get down on your knees and pray for forgiveness."

"Forgiveness of what?" he asked and knew he shouldn't have given her an opening the moment the words were out of his mouth.

"Well, you musta done something to get yourself in this here predicament," she said, adding a "humph" for emphasis.

"You're probably right, Aunt Etta, but that still doesn't explain why you both are here."

"Passed by and saw the cars parked out front, boy," Eddie said, jumping right in. "Thought you folks were having some sort of shindig and didn't invite us."

"Exactly!" Etta said, slipping her arm under Eddie's and jutting out her chin.

"Trust me, there's no party going on."

"So whose Jeep is that?" Eddie demanded.

"And isn't that little Tony's car? What's he doing here? I've never known that boy to get up on Sunday mornings before noon."

"Anthony, uh, spent the night. And, uh, he called

me this morning and asked me to join him for breakfast. You know, a father and son thing," he added, hating that he had to lie to them. He smiled, looking from one skeptical face to the other, hoping that they bought his story.

"Breakfast," Eddie said, his eyes suddenly sparkling. "I could sure use some." He turned to Etta. "How come you never fix me any breakfast?"

"Never!" Etta squealed. "You old fool, I fix you breakfast every morning, just the way you like it." She sucked her teeth in annoyance. "You can't remember a darn thing." She sucked her teeth again and rolled her eyes for good measure.

Eddie scratched his head. "You know, you're right. You sure do." His brows rose when he turned to his nephew. "But I could sure go for a cup of coffee."

"That's right," Etta chimed in. "Where are your manners? Got us standing out in the street like two vagabonds. Your own blood relations. I brought you up better than this." Her eyes welled up as if she was going to cry.

"Now, look what you done, boy. Gone and got your aunt all worked up. All we asked from you was a cup of coffee, but that seems to be too much. And after all we done for ya."

"Oughta be 'shamed, treating your kinfolk like this," Etta said, her voice cracking with emotion.

Dumbfounded, Edward momentarily stood there

totally speechless and wished that the ground would open and swallow him whole. He couldn't believe how the situation had deteriorated to this level in a matter of seconds.

"There's no reason to get upset," he said in his best cajoling voice. "Let's all go inside and I'll make some fresh coffee. I'm sure Denise has some sweet rolls to go with it. How's that sound?"

"Sounds like you finally located your good sense," Etta said and pulled Eddie up the three steps to the front door.

Edward darted around them, stuck his key in the lock, and opened the door.

They stepped in with authority and took a good look around.

"Denise sure keeps a nice place," Etta said, taking off her good church hat with its drooping two-foot, baby blue feather that had seen better days. If Edward remembered correctly, it looked like the same hat she used to wear to church when he was a kid. It had to be the same hat, he concluded, as he watched her place it reverently on the chair. There was no way there could be two of them.

"Make yourselves comfortable. I'll put on the coffee."

"See you finally got the tree up," Eddie commented, opening the buttons on his royal blue shark-skin suit.

"Yes, finally," Edward said.

Etta sniffed. "Christmas just won't be the same this year with you kicked out of the house."

Edward flinched.

"Told you what you need to do, boy, to keep that woman happy," Eddie advised. He patted Etta's thigh. "I know how to keep my woman happy, don't I, baby?" He gave her a wink.

Etta giggled and popped his hand playfully. "You old fool." She leaned over and kissed him on the lips.

Edward smiled at the old couple and hoped that one day when he and Denise were their ages they'd still be able to share those precious loving moments, and still enjoy each other even with all of their quirks and shortcomings. Etta and Eddie may not have had much, but they had each other. That's what was most important. And Edward was willing to give up all that he'd acquired to keep Denise in his life.

He walked into the kitchen and prepared the coffee, then snuck out the back door to check on Anthony and William.

"Everything cool out here?" Edward asked.

"We got it, Dad. How are you making out with the folks?" He wiped sweat from his brow with the back of his hand.

"I think I have them under control. But you're going to have to make an appearance at some point. I told them you spent the night."

"Aw, Dad, can't you make up an excuse?" His handsome face twisted into a grimace. "Aunt Etta is going to quiz me to death about my entire life since birth and Uncle Eddie will want to give me another dance lesson."

William and Edward roared with laughter, feeling the young man's pain.

"Son, if I'm going down, everyone is going down with me," he said, fighting back laughter. "They're really quite harmless."

Anthony cut a look at his father from the corner of his eyes and shook his head in defeat.

"In the meantime, I'd better get back inside before they get suspicious."

Edward returned to the kitchen, poured two cups of coffee, added cream and sugar, took two sweet rolls from the breadbox, and placed everything on a tray.

"Here you go," Edward said, returning to the living room. He set the tray on the coffee table.

Etta picked up her cup and took a testing sip. "Not bad."

"What time is your wife getting home?" Eddie asked.

"About three."

"You plan on being here when she gets in?"

"I, uh, hadn't really thought about it."

"Didn't she put you out?" Etta stated more than asked.

"We just have a difference of opinion at the moment."

"You got more than a difference of opinion. You got two different addresses! You young folks have some strange ways of working things out. Pass me my purse, Eddie."

Eddie handed Etta her purse and she promptly took out her silver flask and splashed a capful in her coffee.

"For my nerves," she muttered, then looked at her nephew. "If you're gonna set around in the woman's house the least you could do is fix dinner so she won't have to be bothered when she gets in."

"Fix dinner?" Edward looked almost frightened. "Dee doesn't like anyone messing around in her kitchen."

"Son, you are about as silly as they come. Of course that's what she says because you've never allowed her to have nothing else around here that she was in control of, except the kitchen!"

"But I . . ."

"Do you want your wife back or not?"

"Yes, ma'am."

"Then act like it." She pushed herself up from the

couch. "Come on, son." She took him by the arm and pulled him into the kitchen. "You just show me where she keeps her ingredients and we'll have dinner cooked up in no time. Watch and learn."

To his amazement, Aunt Etta helped him whip together a wonderful meal in an hour flat. She'd chopped up a bunch of collard greens, tossed in some seasoning, and had them simmering on the stove while Edward diced potatoes, carrots, onions, and celery. Wild rice boiled merrily and after a thorough wash and seasoning, the chicken was roasting in the oven. All the while she made sure Edward paid attention to everything she did. Maybe he should have paid more attention to those cooking shows, he mused, as he checked on the pot of greens.

"You need to do this more often," she said, her voice taking on a soft tone. "Women appreciate things like this." She washed her hands at the sink and wiped them on a yellow-and-white kitchen towel, then turned to her nephew. "That's all any of us want, son, is to be appreciated. If you want a good marriage, it has to be equal. Both of you have to share the load. No roles, no special duties, just equal. Know what I'm sayin'?"

"Yes, ma'am, I think I do."

She patted his cheek. "Good. That's a start. Now get this kitchen cleaned up and me and your uncle are going to be heading home." She started out.

"Aunt Etta . . ."

She turned to him and he leaned down and kissed her cheek. "Thank you."

"Thank me when you get your wife back. Make her want you as much as you claim to want her. Give her some time. She'll come around." With that, she walked out.

Edward thought about his aunt's words of wisdom as he washed utensils and wiped off countertops. Although her choice words of advice only came in spurts, when they did they were well worth listening to.

When Edward returned to the living room, Anthony was sandwiched between Eddie and Etta, taking their usual grilling.

"Dad!" he cried out with much too much enthusiasm, jumping up at the sight of a reprieve. "I was just telling Aunt Etta and Uncle Eddie that I *really* needed to be getting home."

"Sure, son."

"We should be leaving too," Eddie said, rising from his seat. He darted over and helped up his wife.

Etta retrieved her precious hat, setting it at a jaunty angle on her head. "Don't forget what I told you," she said, wagging a finger at Edward while blowing the feather out of her face.

"And make sure you're home by nine," Eddie warned, then turned to Anthony. "You too. Young folks need their rest."

"Yes, sir," Anthony said.

"That chicken should be done in about an hour," Etta said at the door. "Then just turn the oven to warm and it will be just right."

"Thanks, Aunt Etta."

Anthony and Edward waved good-bye as the old couple drove away, the car rattling and clanging down the street.

"Whew," Anthony breathed.

"We better get finished up out back before your mother gets home."

"We've done about as much as we can for today," Anthony said as they headed out back.

William was packing up his tools.

"Wow," Edward said in admiration, looking around. "I'm impressed."

"We still have a lot to do," William said, wiping his hands on his jeans. "But it's a good start. When do you think we can get back in here?"

"I can come by tomorrow and check out what's going on," Anthony offered. "I can always use my laundry as reason for dropping by."

"Good idea," Edward said. "Your mother would never be suspicious about that. Find out what her plans are going to be and then give me a call."

"Will do."

"Okay, fellas, let's cover our tracks and get out of here."

When Denise and Christine returned from brunch, the house was filled with the aroma of Sunday dinner.

"Did you leave the oven on?" Christine asked as they stepped in and closed the door behind them.

"No." Denise put her purse on the foyer table and headed for the kitchen. When she pushed through the kitchen door, she stopped cold. Pots were on the stove and when she pulled the oven open a perfectly browned chicken was in the roasting pan, surrounded by baby potatoes, carrots, and onions.

She stood in the center of her kitchen totally perplexed until she noticed the note on the fridge.

> *Dee,*
> *Just wanted you to know I was thinking of you. I realize you need some time. And I'm willing to give that to you. Enjoy your dinner.*
> > *Love always,*
> > *Ed*

She held the note to her chest and smiled.

Twenty-one

Denise was in a rotten mood. In the days since leaving that wonderful Sunday dinner, Edward ignored her. In the beautiful note he'd left with the food he'd said she needed time and he was going to give it to her, but for how long? When was he going to resume trying to win her back?

Her teeth tore viciously into a slice of toast. The rat. She wished she knew what was going on in his head. One thing she was certain of, was that he was purposefully wearing those skintight jeans to get her all hot and bothered when he dropped by to check on Christine. He knew she liked him in jeans, just as he knew things with Christine and Reese were going great. Reese was stepping up to the plate, courting Christine, sending flowers, taking her out when he was off-duty.

From the conversation with Christine that morning, Denise had learned Reese had finally seen through Loretta. Apparently, she'd come on to him last night at the hospital. After setting her straight he'd called Christine to apologize. He was coming over to dinner tonight. If Denise wasn't mistaken, Christine would be going with him when he left.

Denise's eyes narrowed as she looked at her little bag on the table. Inside was her belly dancing costume. The gold fabric was so sheer it could be pulled through her wedding ring. When she danced for Edward the undergarments would be of the same fabric. Maybe she could work it out so that the next time he came over she'd be practicing with her costume on. She grinned. He'd swallow his tongue.

Her mood brightening, Denise finished the toast and took her breakfast dishes to the sink. She didn't want to be late for her dance class. Tomorrow, December twenty-third, was the last day. She'd need every minute, she thought, as she tried to undulate as her instructor had shown her for the past weeks. Her upper torso went up and down, her stomach didn't budge. But she was determined. She was going to do a little tempting herself.

Grabbing the bag and her purse, she headed for the front door. With all Christine and Reese's things in the garage it was impossible to walk through to the back where her car was parked. Locking the door, she started around the side of the house.

"Mama, wait."

She turned to see Anthony get out of his Acura Legend. He'd always loved her old car and she had given it to him when he was a junior in high school. The gray sports car's paint gleamed. Anthony might not have kept a neat room, but he'd always kept the car in top condition. "Good morning, Anthony."

"Hi, Mama." Popping the trunk, he hauled out a duffle bag stretched to the seams. "I'm going in late this morning and thought I'd bring my laundry over."

Her gaze roamed over his sweat suit. "Going to the gym?"

He grinned. "I got a racquetball match. I'm going to cream Dale."

She placed her hand on his shoulder when he stopped in front of her. He planned on playing while she worked. Her fault. "Anthony, you know I love you, don't you?"

His eyebrows knitted. "Yes, ma'am."

"Then do your own laundry from now on." She removed her hand. "I have an appointment."

"You're serious?" His brown eyes widened. "You're not going to do my laundry?"

She sighed. It had definitely been a mistake to do all the housework so her family would have more leisure time. "No, I'm not. You have to learn how to do things for yourself."

"But I don't know how," he told her.

"I'll be home tonight. Come back and I'll show you, but I won't do it for you." She checked her watch. "Sorry, but I really have to leave."

For a moment Anthony stood there perplexed, then snapped out of it when his mother started walking away. "Where are you going that's so important?"

He sounded so much like his father her eyebrow lifted in annoyance. "I beg your pardon."

Anthony shifted uneasily. "I mean, are you all right, Mama?"

She touched his cheek reassuringly. "Don't worry about me. I'm just going to class."

"Class?"

"Belly dancing."

His mouth fell open.

She held up the small bag. "My costume. Goodbye, honey, see you tonight if you want my help." She almost skipped to the car. She didn't have a doubt where Anthony would go. My, she'd like to be a fly on the wall when he told his father.

"Belly dancing!" Edward yelled, shooting up from his desk.

Anthony shook his head as if he still couldn't believe it. "Daddy, she had this . . . this little bag that she said her costume was in. Daddy, you've got to do something. She's acting strange. I went over there to get the dirt just like we discussed, using my laundry as an excuse to talk to her. I still can't believe she refused this time."

"Her not doing your laundry might be a good idea."

"But Mama has always done it," he said. "Even when I was in college."

Edward stopped, stared at his son, then continued pacing, his hands shoved into his front pockets. "I think your mother has decided we need to learn to do things for ourselves. I think she's right."

Anthony's shoulders slumped. "But it's hard when you've always had it done for you. Nobody takes better care of us than Mama."

Edward's head came up, snatching his hands out of his pockets. "What did you say?"

"Just that it's hard to accept since Mama has always taken such good care of us."

"And we've always taken without any thought of giving." Edward shook his head. Aunt Etta was right again. "How could we, I, have been so selfish?"

"We do things for Mama," Anthony defended.

"Name one," Edward said, his hands on his hips.

Anthony opened his mouth, then closed it. "Jeez."

"Exactly." Edward began to pace again. "It's a wonder she didn't throw us all out sooner."

"Christine is still there."

"Because she has a husband who is, rather was, as thick-headed as we were." Edward stopped and braced a hip on the corner of his desk. "I just hope and pray my plan works. I've got to get my wife back and get her to call off this crazy idea of a divorce. I know she still loves me just as much as I love her."

Anthony grinned. "You asking me for pointers, Daddy?"

Edward almost smiled. "Get out of here and go to work. I'll let you know if I can't handle things."

"Good luck, but if I were you I'd put a stop to that belly dancing." Anthony opened the door. "That costume had to be triple-X rated."

As the door closed Edward visualized Denise in something flimsy with a half veil across her face, her brown eyes promising untold passion, her supple body moving sensuously to the music, her slender arms moving beguilingly. But he wasn't in the picture.

He snatched his coat from the rack. He couldn't get out of his office fast enough. The only man looking at his wife was going to be him.

"Yummy. Now that's what I call tall, dark, and delicious."

"If he were a few years younger I'd like to practice my moves on him."

The two women from Denise's dance class laughed uproariously as they stared at Edward, arms folded, long legs crossed, as he leaned against the hood of his SUV with a lazy grace. Dressed in a denim shirt and blue jeans, Denise had to admit he looked good. The temperature, in the low fifties, didn't seem to bother him.

She might have smacked her lips if he wasn't watching her so intently. She couldn't help but remember all the times in her senior year when, after school was dismissed, she'd come outside and find him waiting in his beat-up car. Edward had always taken care of his own, he just had to learn that his own could take care of themselves.

"Wonder who he's waiting on?" Helen, a divorcée and the more outspoken of the two women, asked.

Denise felt compelled to say, "Me."

Two pairs of slightly envious eyes converged on her.

"You go, girl," they chorused.

Denise didn't know whether to say thanks or tuck her head in embarrassment.

"With a hunk like that, I can see why your outfit is off the chain," said Carrie, a young college student at Grambling. Her stomach was so tight you could probably bounce a dime off of it. "We're still on for tonight?"

Denise nodded, her gaze still on Edward. "I'll see you tonight around seven."

Waving, the women took off in different directions to their cars. Denise was left alone to face the silent man watching her. She stopped about a foot from him, glad she had refreshed her makeup after leaving class and that the cranberry-colored turtleneck she wore complimented her amber complexion. Now that she had Edward's attention, she planned on keeping it. "Good morning, Edward."

" 'Morning, Denise." He didn't move, just continued to watch her.

"Anthony?" she asked, knowing the answer. Her son had certainly been predictable.

He nodded.

"Christine?" she asked.

He nodded again.

Her delight at seeing him began creeping toward annoyance. "My, you're talkative this morning."

"I was listening like you always wanted and thinking how beautiful you are and how blessed and lucky I am to have you for my wife."

Denise felt her throat clog with emotion. Sneaky. Very sneaky and very effective.

Straightening, he pulled her between his legs.

"So, when are you going to give me a demonstration?" His voice was low and inviting.

She'd expected him to blow his top, not practically seduce her in the parking lot. She felt herself melting against him, her body fitting itself to his with a will of its own. It had been so long.

His dark eyes glittered down at her, as if reading her thoughts. "We can be home in twenty minutes."

Mentioning home snapped her out of her sensual haze. Time to get back on track. He'd been doing so well before the note. "The realtor is becoming anxious. You can't keep putting off signing the papers. He said he may have a buyer," she fibbed.

He glowered down at her. "He's wasting his time. That's our house and it's going to remain ours."

"That's debatable," she said, stepping back and slipping her gloved hands into her coat pockets.

"You didn't used to be this stubborn," he said, clearly annoyed.

Denise grinned. "Thank you. Now, if you'll excuse me, I have errands to run." She started down the sidewalk.

He fell into step beside her. "You're going grocery shopping?"

"Yes." She stepped off the sidewalk of the strip shopping center and headed for her car.

He caught her arm. "I could go with you."

Edward had gone grocery shopping with her exactly once, the week they were married. "You'd be bored in five minutes."

His hand slid down her arm to catch her hand. "Not with you, I wouldn't."

She simply stared at him.

He sighed. "Maybe so. Just answer me one question. No evasion, no double questions. I'm ninety-nine-point-nine percent sure I know the answer already, but I need to hear you say it."

"If I can." Realizing it was going to be a very important one, Denise hugged her purse and bag to her chest.

"Do you still love me?"

She stared up at him. Suddenly she felt afraid of what she had started. What if he got tired and walked away? Two hours ago she'd been miserable because he was ignoring her. But if she said yes, would she lose her advantage?

"Dee," he said, and the word seemed torn from him.

She reached for the door handle, but couldn't make herself open the door. "If . . . if I didn't love you, this wouldn't feel like my soul is being ripped from my body."

"Dee." He pulled her around, holding her tightly, desperately. "I . . . I . . ."

She held him just as tightly as he held her. The curious stares of people passing, the biting wind, meant nothing, only this man and this love of a lifetime.

"I may have made you want to pull out my hair, but I've never let you down, have I?" Edward asked.

"No."

He stepped away and stared intently down at her. "I'm going to get you back."

"You better," she threatened, brushing at the moisture pooling at the corner of her eyes.

He looked as if he didn't know whether to laugh or cry. "This new you will take some getting used to."

"Stop complaining, Edward, and go to work," she said, pushing against his chest and opening her door. "I have things to do."

He caught the door before it closed. "Mind if I come over tonight? If you're busy, I can show Anthony how to wash."

The new Edward might take some getting used to as well. "Is this a way of inviting yourself to dinner as well?"

"Am I that obvious?" he said, flashing a smile.

Starting the motor, she activated the window. "Rocking Around the Christmas Tree" played on the radio. "It's gumbo tonight."

He grinned roguishly. "I love gumbo, especially yours."

She grinned back. *Maybe we'll have a chance to*

rock around the Christmas tree together yet. "See you tonight, Edward."

"I'll be there," he said, brushing his hand gently against her cheek. "If you don't mind, could you pay the monthly bills? You know where everything is kept."

Her throat was too full to do anything but nod. From the first day of their marriage, Edward had always kept the checkbook.

"Great." He stepped back. "Drive carefully."

"Good-bye," she finally managed, then drove off, grinning from ear to ear.

Twenty-two

With Denise out of the way for a few hours, Edward darted over to the house to get as much work done as he could before she returned. When he pulled up out front he was surprised when Anthony greeted him at the door.

"Hey, Dad. Did you find Mom?"

"I found her all right," he said, mounting the three steps to the house and imagining his wife in some skimpy outfit.

"And?"

"Let's just say we have a truce—for the moment." He could never admit to his son that he couldn't wait for Denise to show him everything she'd learned.

Anthony frowned. "If you say so."

"What are you doing here anyway?"

"Trying to figure out this laundry thing," he said, looking like a stray puppy.

Edward shook his head and walked inside. He'd

been gone from his house for nearly a month, but it felt like an eternity. He missed the comforts of his home, but more importantly, he missed his wife and what he thought they had together. But he promised himself that when he came back—and he would— he'd be a better man, a wiser man, and the husband that Denise deserved. Each day away from the people and things he held dear offered him a new lesson.

"Well, don't just stand around, let's get busy," Edward said. "No telling what time your mother will be back."

"But what about my laundry?"

"We'll figure it out later." He headed to the back of the house with Anthony trailing behind.

"Dad?" He handed his father a plank.

"Yeah?" Edward expertly measured the surface, then lined up the board.

"I know this might be kind of personal, but are you cool with this belly dancing thing? Don't you think Mom has gone a little too far? I just can't imagine Mom . . . well . . . you know. She's my mother."

Edward worked hard at beating back his laughter, listening to the forlorn tone of his son. The fact of the matter was, kids could never see their parents as sexual beings, just two people who got together long enough to have them.

"What I've come to understand in these past few weeks is that your mom is her own woman. She's entitled to spread her wings and do the things that make her happy, not always working on someone else's happiness and needs—namely ours."

"But . . ."

"It's not as if she's running around town in that outfit or performing for an audience in a club."

"What if she did? 'Cause to be truthful, I don't put anything past her lately."

For a hot second, Edward envisioned Denise on a stage in some dimly lit dive, dancing for a room full of howling men. His blood pressure rose.

"I'm sure your mother wouldn't do something like that," he said, as much to convince his son as himself. "I know your mother." At least he thought he did at one time. But did he now?

Sultry music rang in his head as Denise stepped onto the stage of *The Jerry Springer Show* to reveal to the world her hidden life as a belly dancer for hire. He would sit there appalled as Denise slinked her way across stage, undulating to the beat of the audience's applause.

Suddenly it took all of his willpower to restrain himself from scouring the town, looking for her and demanding that she give up all of her crazy plans and schemes and come back home where she belonged.

"Dad?" Anthony tapped him on the shoulder. "Are you okay?"

Edward blinked and focused on his son. "Yes, fine. Come on, we have work to do. And don't worry. All of this is going to work out. We're going to be one big happy family again, celebrating the best Christmas ever." He wanted to believe that. He had to believe that.

The moment Edward was out of sight Denise pulled the car to the curb. She pulled out her cell phone and called Christine.

" 'Operation Wake-up Call' is working like a charm," she said to her daughter.

"Dad didn't blow a gasket?" she asked, totally surprised.

"Nope. He was quite charming," she said wistfully. "And he actually turned over the bill paying to me. I still can't believe it." She grinned and shook her head in amazement. "Bills and finances were always your father's domain. I think he truly sees that there can be two heads in a household."

"Wow! Maybe I need to take up belly dancing," Christine said, laughing.

Denise chuckled but didn't encourage the idea. "How about just inviting Reese to dinner tonight for starters?"

"That's an idea. I'll give him a call. Do you need anything?"

"No. I'm on my way to the market now. I think I'll ask two of my classmates as well. And maybe even Aunt Etta and Uncle Eddie."

"Now that sounds like a party," Christine said, delight lifting her voice.

"It sure does. See you around seven."

"I'll be there."

Denise hurried over to the market to pick up everything she needed for dinner. She wanted it to be special. With Christmas only days away, the holiday season was finally seeping into her pores.

As she walked up and down the aisles, she couldn't help but smile when she thought about the moment she'd stepped out of class to find Edward waiting for her. At first, from the stern look on his face, she was certain that he was going to insist that she give up her dancing, the same way he'd wanted her to give up her sewing. But he'd surprised her— totally. Not only was he pleasant about the whole thing, he actually wanted a private demonstration.

She giggled, causing a woman coming up the aisle to look at her suspiciously and hurry by, clutching her infant close to her chest.

Ducking her head in mild embarrassment, Denise continued her shopping while thinking about the show she was going to put on for Edward when she got him alone. She was more than determined to be really good at it. She wanted his eyes to roll in the back of his head when he watched her put the moves on him. Just the thought of what would come after her performance sent a surge of heat racing through her body. The moment of truth couldn't come fast enough.

Twenty-three

The house was filled with people, just the way Denise liked it. Impulsively she'd invited Monique and Jeff over to dinner. Christine and Reese were keeping them company, and keeping an eye on the seafood gumbo, while she finished measuring Carrie and Helen.

"That should do it," Denise said as Carrie pulled her black knit sweater back down. It stopped an inch above her belly button. "I'll have them ready by to-morrow for the last day of class."

"So soon?" Helen asked, excitement in her voice.

"I sew fast," Denise said, not wanting to admit they were her only clients. But she planned to change that. "Shall we go back downstairs? I'd like both of you to stay and have dinner with us."

"I was hoping you'd ask," Carrie said and made a face. "The food at the college cafeteria is the pits."

Helen laughed. "How well I remember."

Denise opened the attic door to lead the women to the kitchen. "I never went to college, but my family has stories about the food that will curl your toes."

"Don't get me started," Carrie said.

The women started down the stairs just as Anthony started up. He took one look at Carrie and she at him, and both stopped and stared. Denise sighed and said a silent good-bye to Sherri. "Helen Boyd, Carrie Sims, my son, Anthony."

Anthony remembered his manners, but his interest in Carrie was clear. His gaze kept skipping back to her as he talked to Denise. "If you have time, I'm ready for my first lesson."

"You're going to learn belly dancing?" Carrie asked, with a teasing smile.

"Something much more mundane. Washing my clothes," he answered, smiling back at her.

"Your father is going to help you," Denise said. "In the meantime, why don't you take Carrie to the kitchen? She's staying for dinner."

"Great!" Anthony lightly grasped Carrie's arm and went back down the stairs.

"Can you ever remember being that young and that carefree?" Helen asked.

"As a matter of fact, I can," Denise said as they continued down the stairs. At the landing the doorbell sounded. "Excuse me." The beating of her heart increased with every step. Her hand actually shook as she turned the deadbolt and opened the door. Her gaze flickered from Edward to the two elderly people who pushed past him.

"Get out of the way, boy. My bones are getting cold," Aunt Etta admonished.

"You think the boy would want to get to courting," Uncle Eddie said. "Must have been dropped on his head as a baby, but I don't 'member."

"You don't remember yesterday," his wife said.

"Yes, I do, but I 'member last night better." Grinning, he helped her off with her coat and opened the hall closet door.

Denise stood there with her mouth open until a lean, brown finger lifted her chin. "I can't believe it," she whispered.

Edward sighed. "At least you don't have to listen to them talk about it and you're not getting any."

Denise's cheeks flamed and she shushed Edward.

"Tell the truth and shame the devil," he said with a mischievous grin.

Aunt Etta's head perked up. "Don't talk about the devil in my presence, boy. You'd think we didn't raise you right."

Uncle Eddie shook his graying head. "Must have been dropped and they didn't tell us. Got no sense of decency to come dragging home after everybody trying to sleep. Won't happen again. I'm driving tonight."

Denise put her hand over her mouth until she could control the laughter threatening to bubble out. "We were about to sit down to dinner. You're right on time."

Aunt Etta opened her black patent leather pocketbook. "Got my special sauce."

"Come on, Etta. Let's leave them while you go fix the food." They started for the kitchen.

Denise took off after them, completely ignoring Edward's laughter.

She'd saved her gumbo and, after everyone had eaten, they all moved to the family room. The Christmas tree glittered like spun gold. Looking at her family, Denise glanced at the angel on top of the tree again and felt Edward's hand on her shoulder.

"We'll make it," he whispered in her ear.

"Stop that, boy," Uncle Eddie said from the comfort of Edward's favorite chair. "Time and place for everything."

Denise heard a distinct growl from Edward. Her lips twitched. "Coffee or soft drinks anyone?" She glanced at Monique. "Or in your case, tea?"

"I'm fine and stuffed," she said, reaching out her hand for her husband's, which he immediately took.

"Thank you for inviting us," Jeff said from his seat on the floor by his wife. "I'm not the best cook and we both were getting tired of takeout."

"How well I remember," Denise said. "I'll bring over a dish tomorrow." The young couple quickly started to protest, but she talked over them. "I'll just make a little extra."

"Don't argue with her, Jeff and Monique." Edward placed his hand back on his wife's shoulder. "She takes care of those she cares about."

"That's the way it should be," Aunt Etta said from across the room. "What time is it getting to be?"

"Eight-ten," came the answer from Reese and Jeff. A muscle ticked in Edward's temple. Christine and Anthony looked at their father in sympathy.

Folding her hands back over her wide girth, Aunt Etta leaned back in the easy chair.

Carrie rose. "I better get going. My first class is at eight. Thank you for dinner, Denise. I can't wait to see the belly dancing costume you're making for me."

Edward gave Denise a look, but didn't say anything, for which she was thankful. She certainly didn't want a scene in front of her friends.

Helen came to her feet as well. "Denise has the sexiest outfit in class."

Uncle Eddie jerked upright. "Denise is taking a sex class? Edward, boy, you need to put your foot down!"

Christine quickly walked over to the agitated older man and put a comforting arm around his thin shoulders. "No, Uncle Eddie, Mama is not taking a sex class."

"She better not be or I won't let that boy come courting anymore," he said.

There was a stunned silence for a moment, then a lot of clearing of throats and coughing. Edward groaned and covered his face with both hands.

"I'll show you to the door," Denise said, her mouth twitching.

Anthony hopped up from his seat beside her. "I'll go with you, Mama."

Denise had expected as much as she showed Helen and Carrie to the door, then watched Anthony walk Carrie to her car. Wanting to give them some privacy, she came back inside as soon as Helen drove off.

She was just in time to see Jeff help Monique to her feet. "I'm glad you could come over. I'll bring the dinner over tomorrow around five," she told them.

"Thank you," they both said and in seconds they were gone.

"I guess I better get going as well. Early day tomorrow." Reese looked pointedly at Christine. "I'm off tomorrow night. I made reservations at your favorite restaurant. Or we could have dinner at home? I could cook."

"Why don't we talk about it tonight . . . at home?" Christine said.

He whooped, then grabbed Christine, his voice trembling as much as his body when he said, "I love you." He leaned her away and stared down into her face. "I was an idiot not to listen to you. It'll never happen again. I promise you that."

Christine kissed him gently on the lips. "Let's go home."

Grinning broadly, Reese ushered his wife toward the door. "We'll pick up Christine's things tomorrow."

"Good night," Denise and Edward said as the young couple hurried from the house.

"They're deserting this place like rats on a sinkin' ship," Uncle Eddie said as he came slowly to his feet. "We better go, too."

"I'm staying to help Anthony," Edward told him. "He can drop me off."

"He shouldn't be out late either." Aunt Etta stuck her pocketbook beneath her arm. "Get your coat and let's go."

Edward leaned back on the sofa and folded his arms across his chest. "I'm not going."

"Now see here, as long as you're under my roof, you'll abide by my rules." Uncle Eddie walked over to Edward and stared mutinously down at him.

"He can spend the night," Denise heard herself say. Edward loved his aunt and uncle, but they'd try the patience of a saint.

They all stared at her. "He's going to help Anthony do his laundry while I do some sewing. I'll see that he goes to bed when he's finished."

Her eccentric in-laws grinned at each other, and then Uncle Eddie slapped Edward on the shoulder with surprising strength and winked. "Don't forget what I told you."

Denise didn't want to think about what he might have told Edward or if she'd been had. She quickly got their coats. She didn't breathe easier until they drove away. Carrie pulled off behind them.

"You want Anthony and me to help you with the kitchen?" Edward asked.

She was no longer surprised by his offer to help, but she felt strangely nervous. "I wrote out the bills and plan to mail them in the morning."

"I never doubted," he said. "You're a remarkable woman, Denise."

"Well." She moistened her lips. "Anthony, your father is going to help you. I'm going up to my sewing room." Denise didn't think of her quick escape as cowardly, just a strategic retreat. But how was she going to deal with Edward under the same roof and not in the same bed?

Twenty-four

With everyone gone, it was finally just the two of them. But not the way Edward imagined. He flipped onto his side in the narrow single bed, careful not to find himself on the floor.

Less than ten feet away was his beautiful wife. The only thing that separated them was an inlaid wood door that he could easily plow his way through with a shove of his shoulder. He flipped onto his other side and stared at the wall. Suddenly an image of Denise clothed in nothing more than a sheer miniskirt and bra-like top appeared in front of him with jingle bells dangling from every tempting location. The room became suddenly warm and he threw the light blanket off of him.

"This is ridiculous." He got up and headed out into the hall. The house was silent. He could hear the crickets outside the hall window. He tiptoed down the hall and pressed his ear to the bedroom door. Silence. *What would she do if I came in and slipped in between the sheets?* he wondered when the sudden flash of Denise wielding that nail file popped into his head. He exhaled a deep breath.

Ravishing his wife was not the answer, he realized. Sex was not their problem, it never had been. Denise admitted as much. It was more than that. It was him learning to respect and accept her as not simply an object for his desires or to fulfill his needs and the needs of their family, but as a whole woman. That's what she had been asking for all along. And maybe it took these past weeks, experiencing the thought of losing her, of being without her, to finally help him to understand that fully. She didn't need him to just make love to her, she needed him to be *in* love with her, to romance her and make her feel like the bride he married.

Smiling, he turned away and returned to the single bed alone.

Denise stared up at the ceiling, counting the sheep that skipped merrily across the off-white surface. She turned toward her closed bedroom door and wondered if Edward was just as restless as she. She kicked off the covers, got up, and made her way across the darkened room. Inching the door open, she peeked out into the hallway. A sliver of moonlight could be seen coming from behind Edward's partially opened door.

Easing down the hallway, she stopped short of the door, listening for any movement. Edward's deep snores greeted her. Her heart sunk to her feet. Here she was driving herself crazy with wanting him and he slept as soundly as a babe. Fine! If he could sleep so could she.

Marching back into her room she practically threw herself into her bed. By the time she drifted off into a fitful sleep, the sun was cresting over the horizon. *The best-laid plans,* was her last tormented thought before her eyes finally closed.

By the time she awoke the following morning, it was nearly ten. She jumped up from bed and hurried down the hallway. Edward's room was empty, the bed was neatly made. Sighing, she slowly returned to her room to straighten up. *All he needed was a place to sleep*, she thought miserably as she pulled the sheets from the bed and replaced them with fresh ones. That mundane task completed, she took her shower, dressed, and went downstairs with the intention of fixing a light breakfast before tackling the task of finishing the costumes for her classmates.

But when she entered the kitchen she couldn't have been more surprised than if Santa had been sitting there to greet her.

On the table was a perfect place setting for two, with a single rose in a slender crystal vase. Braced against the vase was a note:

> Dee,
> I thought you needed your rest so I took the liberty of trying my hand at breakfast. I hope I didn't leave too much of a mess. Your food is in the warmer in the oven. I know the place setting is for two because I wanted you to think of me as sharing this morning with you, as I hope we will share many more together. It would give me great joy if you would be my date for tonight for a Christmas Eve dinner. If your answer is yes, I'll pick you up at seven-thirty. You know my number.
>
> Love, Ed

Denise beamed with delight and did a great imitation of James Brown across her kitchen floor. Coming up short, she realized she had tons of things to do before her date. A date—with her husband!

Quickly eating her breakfast, which wasn't bad, she cleaned up the kitchen and darted upstairs to the attic to finish the costumes. Her class was at 3:00 to-

day and if she hurried she could stop at the hair salon for a touch-up and a rinse afterward. She wanted
to look extra-special tonight. Before she left the
house, she called Ed's office only to find out that he
was out on a job.

"Can I transfer you to his voicemail, Mrs. Morrison?" Lena, his secretary, asked.

"That's okay, Lena, I'll call his cell phone.
Thanks." She hung up, then dialed his cell.

"Morrison," he answered on the first ring.

"Seven-thirty sounds fine," she said softly.

"I'll be there with bells on."

"I'll be waiting." Slowly she hung up the phone
and her heart beat with the same anticipation it did
when she would sit by the window waiting for him
to pick her up in the early days of their courtship.
Old folks often said you couldn't go back, but
maybe she could prove them wrong. In the meantime she had work to do.

Class flew by and Carrie and Helen were thrilled with
their outfits, and couldn't compliment her enough on
the wonderful job she'd done, especially in such a
short period of time. Thanking them profusely, she
darted over to the hair salon and went into a mild
panic when she was informed that the wait would be
at least an hour before they could get to her. While she

waited she decided to get a manicure and a pedicure. Why not? she reasoned. Tonight was special. Finally she was in the chair and a bit more than an hour later she looked into the mirror and was thrilled with what the stylist had done. A little cut, a little rinse, and she looked ten years younger. The woman insisted on arching her brows as well, which highlighted her almond-shaped eyes. With a little more than an hour to spare, she darted home and got ready for her date.

She was just applying the last touches of her makeup when the doorbell rang. Willing her heart to be still, she took a deep breath and slowly descended the stairs. But when she opened the door, her breath caught in her chest.

Edward Morrison looked like one of those mature male models from the catalogues. Always a handsome and fit man, he was even more dashing in his midnight blue suit, matching tie, and pale blue shirt. From the looks of him, he'd been to the barber for a perfect shave and shape-up, his dark hair sprinkled with gray cut close to his head.

"You look beautiful," he said, and leaned down to kiss her chastely on her cheek. "You always did look good in red."

She'd decided on her red velvet sheath with the cowl neckline, cinched waist, and body-hugging length. It hit her just above the knees and she knew that Edward always had a thing for her legs.

"You're looking quite gorgeous yourself," she said, smiling like an infatuated teen.

"Ready?"

She nodded briskly. "Let me just get my jacket." She took her matching jacket from the chair in the hall and picked up her purse.

"Let me help you with that."

He eased the jacket around her shoulders and she shivered when she felt his warm breath against her neck and his fingers gently pressing into her flesh. For a hot minute, she thought about calling the whole night off and just taking him upstairs and having her way with him. But his voice in her ear jolted her out of her daydream.

"The car is out front."

When she stepped outside she was momentarily confused. She turned to him. "Where's your car?"

"I decided that I would rent a car for us tonight so that I could concentrate on you and not on driving."

The chauffeur stepped out and opened the door for them.

"After you," Edward said, helping her into the car.

Denise thought she was in a dream, but if she was she didn't want to wake up anytime soon.

Edward had selected an exquisite Italian restaurant just outside the city limits. And when Denise looked around everything came rushing back. It was the same restaurant he'd brought her to when he proposed. As the waiter showed them to their table she promised herself that she wouldn't cry.

"Do you remember?" Edward asked once they were seated.

Against her will, her eyes filled and she dabbed at them with the linen napkin. "Yes," she whispered.

He reached across the table and took her hand, slipped off her wedding band and engagement ring, and placed each one in a box that he pulled from his jacket pocket. He placed both of them on the table between them.

"Twenty-seven years ago," he began, "I asked you to be my wife. We had visions of being together happily ever after. Somewhere along the way, we hit a detour. Or maybe I did. I started to believe that things, possessions, and control were what made a marriage work. It took the thought of losing you, Denise, to make me finally understand that marriage is so much more than that."

"Ed . . . I . . ."

"Wait, let me finish. Somewhere along the line, the romance disappeared, the courting, the fun, and the partnership. In the beginning, we struggled together. All we had was each other, a little one-bedroom apartment, and a black-and-white television." They both chuckled. "Now we have more than any couple could ask for, but we lost each other along the way. You gave me everything I needed to make me strong, but I didn't do the same for you. It may take me some time, but I want to work on fixing that. I want to hold onto these rings and present them to you when I'm the man you deserve to call husband. If you can be patient, I'll make it happen. If you know nothing else about me, you know I'm determined."

Denise didn't know what to say. On the one hand, she was thrilled that at least on the surface Edward truly seemed set on making the marriage work and allowing her to be an important part of it. But on the other hand, she was terrified, terrified that this could very well be the end. He'd taken back the very symbol that bound them together. She had to think. But she couldn't. Instead she tried to focus on her meal, which began to taste like sawdust.

She wasn't sure how long the dinner lasted or what it was that they talked about. Her mind was sludge. Absently, she kept touching her bare fingers and another surge of dread would tramp through her.

At some point the night finally came to an end as the driver pulled up in front of their house. Desperate, Denise gave it one last effort, the one thing that Edward had never been able to resist—her.

Standing in the doorway she suddenly felt like an awkward teenager on a first date deciding if this would be the night. But a part of her deeply believed that if it wasn't, she might truly lose her husband for good.

"Uh, it's getting really late," she said, looking up into his eyes. "Why . . . don't you spend the night? I could make us some coffee . . . we could talk." She wanted to touch him, but dared not.

Edward gave her a half smile, then leaned down and kissed her lightly on the lips. "I don't think that would be such a great idea, especially on a first date. You wanted a new me and the first thing on my list is to respect you. So in light of that, I'm going to head over to my aunt and uncle's and try to get some sleep. I hope it's okay if I stop over tomorrow and open the gifts with the family."

She swallowed down the lump in her throat. "Of . . . course."

He smiled gently. "Good night, Denise."

"Good night." She stood there for several unbelievably long moments as she watched the limo whisk him away.

Slowly she turned away and closed the door, letting the tears she'd held onto for hours flow down her cheeks.

Twenty-five

She was alone Christmas Eve and it was her fault. Huddled on the four-poster she'd once shared with Edward, Denise fought a losing battle to keep tears from streaming down her cheeks. She ached so badly she didn't know if she could stand it. The house was silent instead of ringing with the joyous laughter of years past.

My fault.

Hugging a throw pillow to her stomach, she drew her knees up toward her chest. Her finger kept running over the empty space where her wedding rings had once been. Edward had worked an extra job to buy her the fourth-of-a-carat diamond. The symbol of their love had mattered more than the size of the stone, and he had taken her rings from her hand.

The only thing that gave her any hope was that Edward hadn't taken off his wedding band. He'd also explained his reasoning, but it was hard to accept with her alone in bed and aching for her husband.

In the past weeks since she'd asked for a divorce, he'd shown he understood her need for independence and to be an active part of the decision making for them. He had become the partner she wanted, but he wasn't there with her.

Her Christmas miracle wasn't going to happen.

Denise woke with a splitting headache and eyes that felt gritty as sandpaper. The throw pillow was still clasped tightly to her chest. As usual, she was on Edward's side of the bed.

It was Christmas Day. People everywhere were celebrating with family and friends. All she wanted to do was pull the covers back over her head and try to block out the impossible mess she'd made of her marriage.

Half a loaf is better than none. Too late. Much too late.

Opening her eyes, she sat up on the side of the bed. She couldn't wallow in misery all day. Christine and Anthony would come by. Maybe they'd take the food she'd cooked, thinking there would be a celebration.

Foolish woman. Making herself stand, she went to the shower.

. . .

Thirty minutes later, Denise slowly went down the stairs. She hadn't meant to, but her eyes went almost accusingly to the Christmas tree. Her brow knitted on seeing it lit. She distinctly remembered unplugging it last night. Still frowning, she walked over.

Her eyes widened as she saw a note dangling from the hand of the angel. *Merry Christmas. Look for a slender gold-wrapped box.*

Her heart thudding, she dropped to her knees, prepared to throw all the carefully wrapped packages aside if need be. But there it was, on top. Her hands shaking, she tore the paper off, then gasped on seeing the gold nameplate: DENISE K. MORRISON, DESIGNER. She was so shaken she almost missed the note underneath that said, *Look in the bottom cabinet in the kitchen.*

Springing up, she raced to the kitchen to throw open door after door until she saw it—bolt after bolt of fabric. Dangling from the top was another note. *Pick up your next gift in the garage.*

Shooting upward, she whirled and was off again. Her hand was shaking so badly she could hardly open the door. Then, when she did, she burst into tears.

"Merry Christmas, Dee."

"Merry Christmas, Mama."

"Merry Christmas, Mrs. Morrison."

She could hardly take it all in. Her family and in-laws stood in the middle of a newly constructed sewing salon equipped with state-of-the-art equipment.

"When . . . how—" she stammered.

Edward stepped forward and pulled her into his arms. "Whenever you were out of the house."

"You really do understand." She blinked back tears of happiness.

"Finally," he said. "I'm sorry for all those years I heard but never really listened. All I ever wanted was for you to be happy."

She gazed up at him with complete love and devotion. "I know that now. I guess I just needed to hear the words."

"I love you, Denise Morrison. You're the most wonderful, the most beautiful, the sexiest woman in the world to me, and I will do whatever it takes to remind you of that every day."

"So will we," the children chorused. "All except the sexy part."

"Sex is the best part," Uncle Eddie said with an emphatic nod of his graying head. "Told the boy that."

Everyone laughed. Denise leaned against Edward, then straightened. "Your chair! Your chair is out here!"

"While you are out here working, I thought I'd keep you company sometime."

Her hands palmed his face. "You won't miss your television programs?"

His hands covered hers. "I'd miss you more."

Denise kissed him.

"I think the boy finally got it," Aunt Etta said. "About time. I'm hungry and I want to see what I got under that big tree."

"I ain't eating no tree," Uncle Eddie said, following her inside.

Laughing, the family followed. Soon the house rang with love and good cheer, and the rocking sounds of James Brown.

While the family was making merry in the living room and tearing through the brightly wrapped gifts, Denise pulled Edward aside.

He wrapped his arms around her waist and pulled her close. "Merry Christmas, baby."

"Merry Christmas. I have something special for you, too."

"Really?"

"Yes. Follow me." She took him by the hand and led him upstairs and into their bedroom. "You sit right there and don't move."

"Your wish is my command."

She darted out of the room and into the attic. Moments later, she returned and got the reaction she'd dreamed of. Edward's eyes really did roll back in his head.

Remembering the moves she'd learned in class, Denise rotated her belly and shimmied her hips, all to the beat that danced in her head.

Edward's mouth dropped open as the exotic moves set off the tiny bells on her skimpy costume signaling her approach. This was better than he'd imagined and he couldn't wait until he could get to what was beneath.

"This is the dance for lovers," she whispered from behind her veil. She reached out for him and pulled him to his feet, then placed her hands on his waist. "Follow me," she instructed.

Laughing and giggling, Edward did an admirable job of matching her beat for beat, until their bodies were pressed against each other, dancing to a rhythm all their own. Piece by piece the sheer fabric fell away from Denise's body, followed by Edward's clothing, which all wound up in a pile at their feet.

"Can I take the lead now?" he whispered in her ear.

"I was hoping you'd say that."

Taking her in his arms he placed her on the bed, gently, like the precious jewel that she was. Looking down into her eyes, he knew that there was no better Christmas gift than the one she would give him. He leaned over the side of the bed and pulled the little black boxes from his pants pocket. Bracing his weight on his elbow, he opened the boxes. One at a time he lifted the rings from their cushioned cases.

"I truly believe that I'm the man you need and want in your life. And if you think that's true too, then I pray you will accept these rings as a token of my love and respect for you and consent to be my wife, my partner, from this day forward."

Tears of complete joy spilled from her eyes as she looked at the unbroken circles that he offered.

"Always and forever," she said through her sobs.

Edward took her hand in his and slipped the rings back onto their rightful place. And, taking as much time as his willpower allowed, he tried to show her with every touch, every dip of his body into hers, how special she was, how important, and how much he deeply loved her.

Her cries of joy were muffled by the sounds of music and laughter bubbling up from downstairs. As she held her husband close, she smiled, realizing that miracles still did happen. She and Edward would be rockin' around the Christmas tree for many years to come!

Take a sneak peek at Donna Hill's
thrilling upcoming hardcover

GETTING HERS

A delicious tale of friendship and revenge

Coming from St. Martin's Press
FEBRUARY 2005

Prologue—
Fate is a Funny Thing

"Dearly beloved, we are gathered here today to put to rest the body of our brother, Troy Benning, husband of Kimberly Sheppard-Benning and a friend to many . . ."

Kim's alabaster complexion was dutifully shielded behind the black veil that dipped down dramatically from her wide-brimmed black hat. She brought a white handkerchief beneath the veil and dabbed at her dry eyes. "Bastard," she muttered.

Tess McDonald cut her dark brown eyes in Kim's direction. She lowered her head. "Careful," she whispered as she feigned looking into her purse. She raised her head and snapped the bag shut.

"Amen," Nicole Perez murmured along with the mourners and clasped Kim's shoulder, with a black-gloved hand in a gesture of support. "And good riddance," she added under her breath.

The good reverend droned on about what a wonderful man Troy was and an endless stream of grievers marched up to the grave to toss a rose or utter words of sorrow and condolence to Kim.

Kim scanned the crowd from behind her veil, hoping to catch a glimpse of Stephanie. Finally she spotted her, with her arm tucked through that of her husband, Malcolm. Kim's stomach muscles tightened as Stephanie's green-eyed gaze found Kim's blue one. Stephanie offered a slow, sad smile before looking away.

Tess desperately wanted a cigarette. Funerals, cops, pre-dawn phone calls, hot sex, and situations out of her control always elevated her craving. Casually she scanned the crowd. There was always a face in the crowd of a funeral that stood out that you knew was not supposed to be there. And when she found that face a few hundred feet away, nearly shadowed by a tree, her heart stumbled in her chest. What was Vincent doing here?

Nicole clasped her gloved hands together and licked her blood-red lips. If only she could get her pulse to slow down and that mad fluttering in her belly to quit. Her onyx eyes darted around the throng of mourners, then returned to rest on the hole in the ground. She swallowed. With all of the situations that she'd found herself in, even behind bars, she hadn't been afraid—wary maybe, cautious for sure, but never afraid. But now, for the first time in her life, she was afraid, scared. She put on a good front, she had to. There was no way that anyone could ever find out what she'd done. If so . . . she didn't want to think about it. She swallowed hard and tugged in a deep breath. This would all be over soon and the three of them could move on with their lives—whatever that may be.

Two Weeks Later:
Tess, Nikki, and Kim raised their glasses in a toast.

"To us," Tess said, as her lids lowered ever so slightly over her honey-brown eyes and the curve of her wide mouth spread in a salacious grin, the bold red color matching her body-hugging designer sheath to perfection.

The trio clinked their flutes together as soft music played in the background. Tuxedoed waiters moved soundlessly around the posh Red Room on the Upper East Side of Manhattan, removing dishes and refilling drinks, while being totally unobtrusive to their elite clientele.

Expertly coiffed as usual, Kim's signature diamond studs sparkled against the light. "I couldn't have done it without you two." She took a sip of her champagne.

"You got that right." Nikki tossed her mane of ink-black hair over her shoulder. Her charcoal eyes snapped with mischief.

They laughed.

"We're not quite done. The pieces are all there; they simply need to be put in place." Tess set down her glass and looked from one woman to the other.

Kim lowered her head and her voice to a whisper. "I still can't believe it."

"What's not to believe? They tried to screw us and we fucked them first," Nicole said with a nonchalant flick of her wrist. Her tennis bracelet flashed.

Kim flushed crimson. She spoke from between clenched teeth. "Do you always have to talk like that?" Her blue eyes darted around the room to see if anyone in earshot was offended. "We can dress you up but we still can't take you out. Are you sure you didn't put a hit out on Troy? I don't put anything past you, Nikki."

Nicole grinned. "A girl is entitled to some secrets." She turned to Tess and shrugged. "What if I did?" She gave Kim a wink. "Be careful, my little pretty, the wife is always the first suspect."

"Nikki—"

Tess stretched her manicured hand across the table and covered Kim's pale fingers with her cocoa-brown ones. "Relax. You know Nikki is just being Nikki. She loves to see you flustered, and you go for it every time."

Kim cut a look in Nicole's direction. Nicole smirked into her glass.

Tess leaned back and looked at her two unlikely friends. Over the past few months they'd gone from virtual strangers and wary adversaries to partners in crime—so to speak—uncovering and revealing some of their deepest secrets and darkest fears. They were a whisper away from tumbling some of the highest powers in government to corporate America to the neighborhood G-Man. It had been risky. They'd put their families, their money, and themselves in jeopardy. It had taken all of their connections, but mostly the irrefutable pact that they had made to get as far as they did. It had been worth the sleepless nights. And when the last piece was dropped in place, Tess might even get what she'd wanted most.

Under normal circumstances they would have never met in a million years—a black, high-priced madam who ran the biggest escort service on the East Coast; a Latina beauty boasting a mouth like a longshoreman, with a penchant for guns and fast cars; and a white, married business icon who was in love with the wife of a congressman. But fate, the stars, law enforcement, and mutual goals had brought them together one fateful afternoon in June that set in motion an elaborate plan of revenge that would change their lives forever.

Francis Ray returns with

THE GRAYSONS!

Take a sneak peek at her upcoming romance

YOU AND NO OTHER

Morgan Grayson's story

Coming from St. Martin's Paperbacks
MARCH 2005

Morgan Grayson was in serious trouble.

Long, elegant fingers tapped out a synchronized beat on the steering wheel of his two-seater sports car to Aretha Franklin's unmistakable voice demanding respect. Morgan knew just how the lady felt.

Easing around the slow-moving Suburban, Morgan resisted the urge to press his foot down on the accelerator and take some of his growing frustrations out with a fast drive. The twisting roads beneath the San De Cristo Mountains outside of Santa Fe were unforgiving when it came to fools and speeding vehicles. Morgan wasn't a fool so he contented himself by increasing the volume of the CD and returned to pondering his problem.

His loving, stubborn, matchmaking mother.

Ruth Grayson had singled him out as the next one of her children to marry off. After she'd thrown Shelby in his path two weeks ago at Luke's wedding, Morgan had erroneously thought she'd need a little more time to regroup. After all, she had enlisted the help of her friends and associates from around the country in looking for a wife for Luke. Knowing she was too sensitive to thrust the same women at him any time soon,

Morgan thought he was safe. But she had outwitted him.

For him she was staying local.

Last week when he'd picked up his dry cleaning, he'd even heard there was a jackpot—a little something so the lucky winner could have a blowout bachelorette party. This morning he had stopped by his mother's house for breakfast and three of her single female colleagues from the University of St. Johns, where she taught music in the graduate program, were there. You'd think his mother would be subtler or that the women would have more pride. No way! They all acted as if this were some type of game. Unfortunately, he was the prize.

His mother had married off Luke, just as she predicted. As the second-born, Morgan was next. In the past he had always been pleased that he was next in line. No longer. Pierce, Brandon, and Sierra were constantly urging him to hold out. *Demanding* might be a more apt word. His younger brothers and sister didn't have to worry. He had no intention of getting married.

He was happy for Luke, and Catherine was a fantastic woman, but marriage wasn't in his plans. His law practice was his mistress, and he liked it that way. The woman hadn't been born who would make him even think about getting serious. But his mother wasn't listening to him.

His fingers flexed on the steering wheel as he wondered how Luke had coped, but since he and Catherine had been holed up in his mountain cabin since they returned a few days ago from their honeymoon in Bali, Morgan couldn't ask him. Probably just as well, Morgan thought as he came over a rise and saw the black iron gate of the Hendersons' ranch that signaled he was almost at his destination. Luke was an unwanted reminder that their mother had been right in her choice for her first-born.

Slowing down, Morgan turned into the paved driveway and saw the white stucco ranch house at the end of the winding, mile-long road. The red-tiled roof gleamed in the bright morning sunlight. The aspen leaves were thick and shimmering with life, the air scented with the last, lingering scents of wildflowers. It was a beautiful fall day. Too bad he couldn't enjoy it.

Stopping in the circular driveway in front of the heavily carved, red double doors, he cut the motor. The BMW roadster purred to a polite silence. He smiled. He'd always been a sucker for cars. He enjoyed the finer things in life and worked long, demanding hours in a job he loved to afford them. With his law practice thriving, his life was perfect in every way but one. His mother.

Thrusting his mother's matchmaking schemes from his mind, Morgan picked up the hand-stitched, leather attaché case from the seat beside him and got out. He had business to take care of. Besides, he could handle any woman she pushed in his path.

Closing the door, he started up the walkway lined with purple sage. The neigh of a horse followed by the throaty laughter of a woman caused him to pause and turn toward the sound. He was just in time to see an elegantly shaped woman take a huge roan stallion smoothly over one six-foot rail, then another. Since Morgan had a fondness for women and horses, he watched the riveting combination of grace and beauty.

The woman's long legs were encased in tan jappours pressed tightly against the animal's gleaming flanks as she guided him over another obstacle. It took strength, skill, and control to handle such a big, powerful animal and to make it appear effortless. Morgan idly wondered if the woman was that controlled in bed or if she was as wild and tantalizing as her laughter had been.

"Excuse me, sir. May I help you?"

The heavily accented voice effectively ended Morgan's speculations and his idle thought of finding out. Pleasure never outweighed business. Pushing the woman from his mind, he turned.

"Yes, I'm Morgan Grayson. I'm here to see Mr. Duval. He's expecting me."

The dark, austure face of the elderly servant dressed in unrelieved black became no less stern at Morgan's announcement. His closely cropped head of gray hair inclined slightly. "Yes, Mr. Grayson. Mr. Duval is expecting you. This way, please."

Morgan followed the man, his gait slow and deliberate, inside the rambling one-story ranch house. The interior was cool, the furniture sleek and ultra-modern. Morgan knew that the couple owned the house, but seldom lived there. They preferred the Mediterrean this time of year and saw the house as a tax write-off. Thanks to the investment advice of his brother, Pierce, they were able to enjoy their retirement in style.

Crossing the slate gray–carpeted floor, the servant knocked briefly on the heavily carved mahogany door. "Mr. Duval. Mr. Grayson is here."

"Send him in," commanded a curt male voice.

"Yes, sir." Opening the door, the servant closed it as soon as Morgan walked through. Morgan saw Andre Duval turn from looking out the window, then take a seat behind his desk. Not by word or look did he acknowledge Morgan. Thankful that his business with Duval would be brief, Morgan crossed the polished oak floor and extended his hand.

"Good afternoon, Mr. Duval. It's a pleasure to meet you." He didn't even wince at the lie.

Duval ignored the hand and stared unflinchingly back at Morgan. "You're late."

Morgan's own eyes narrowed. He'd heard that Duval, a renowned sculptor, was temperamental. Apparently he was also rude. Slowly Morgan twisted the hand he had extended and glanced at the face of the 18-karat Rolex on his wrist. "I'm seven and a half minutes early."

"Where are the papers I'm to sign?"

Not even by a flicker of his thick lashes did Morgan show his irritation. If Duval were his client, he'd walk. He wasn't. He was the client of the Lawson & Lawson law firm in Boston. Kendrick Lawson, the senior partner, had been Morgan's mentor as well as his boss when he attended Harvard. He was now a good friend. Morgan respected and liked the crafty Lawson too much to disappoint him. His firm would get a sizable commission once Duval signed the contract to have *Courage*, his best work thus far, reproduced for limited editions. Besides, a lawyer learned early to deal with unpleasant people and unavoidable situations.

"May I?" Morgan asked, lifting the briefcase over the highly polished surface of the immaculate desk.

The affirmative nod from Duval was curt.

Placing the case on the desk, Morgan opened it and handed the two contracts to Duval. A black-gloved right hand emerged from beneath the desk, took the papers, and laid them carelessly aside. Cold brown eyes never left Morgan's face.

"You can leave now."

The lock snapped shut with a distinctive click. "If you have any questions I'd be happy to answer them. I understood you were expected to sign today and I could overnight them to Mr. Lawson."

"You understood wrong." Duval stood. His left

hand was already in the coat pocket of his loosely constructed black jacket. He slipped his right into the
other pocket. "Good-bye."

Morgan knew when he had been dismissed. He
pulled a card from inside the jacket of his wheat-
colored suit and placed it in the middle of the desk. "If
you need to reach me. Good-bye." Lifting the briefcase
off the desk, he turned to leave.

A brief knock sounded on the door before it swung
open. Bubbling laughter preceded the striking young
woman into the study. "Andre—" She stopped her
headlong dash, her smoky gray eyes widening on seeing Morgan. For a long moment she simply stared.

Morgan was doing the same. She was even more exquisite up close. "Hello."

"Hello," she murmured a bit breathlessly, then
turned to Andre. "I'm sorry. I came in the back from
the stable. I didn't know you had a guest."

"No matter, my dear. Mr. Grayson was just leaving."

Morgan noted Duval's voice had lost its sharpness
and now was almost crooning. Morgan could well understand why. If the woman's whisky voice didn't get
you, the smoky gray eyes and pouting lips would. She
had the kind of face that a man would go to his grave
remembering, and a lush, curvaceous body created to
satisfy any fantasy.

She flushed beneath her golden skin at his open ap-
praisal. All that sex appeal and she could still blush.
Innocence and carnality, an alluring and dangerous combination. Was she "La Flame", the mysterious woman
reported to be the inspiration and reason for Duval's
sculptured pieces to have regained their fire and vitality
after a two-year absence from the art world? It would
certainly explain his rush to get rid of Morgan.

Duval had an unimpeded view of the front of the

house and the stable from the window in his study. It was safe to assume he had seen Morgan watching the young, vibrant woman and hadn't approved.

Morgan smiled. Living on the edge kept a man sharp. "Mr. Duval, I didn't know you had a daughter."

"I don't," Andre snapped.

A smile tugging the corners of her lush mouth, the woman came further into the room. "I think Mr. Grayson is teasing, Andre."

"Phoenix, Morgan Grayson," Andre said grudgingly, obviously annoyed at having to do so.

"Hello, Mr. Grayson."

Morgan's large hand closed over her small delicate one, and he noted the slight roughness of her palms. The unexpected contrast pleased him almost as much as the slight leap in her pulse at the base of her throat, the widening of her beautiful eyes. "Hello, Phoenix."

Moistening her lips, she withdrew her hand. He'd bet the farm that she wasn't the nervous type. Interesting. "Would you like something to drink?" she asked, her voice a fraction huskier than it had been.

Very interesting. "No—"

"Thank you, dear, but Mr. Grayson was just leaving," Andre interrupted. "Besides, you need to change after riding."

Embarrassment replaced the warmth in her face. Her hand fluttered across the front of her wrinkled white blouse, then down the side of her dusty jappours. "Please excuse my appearance. I was so excited about Crimson settling in so well, I didn't think."

Morgan's own smile increased to put her at ease. Twin dimples he had always detested winked. "No apology needed. It was a pleasure watching you ride."

The corners of her very tempting mouth curved upward again. "Crimson did all the work."

"Since I ride, I know better."

"Phoenix," Andre called, his voice tight. "You really need to change out of those clothes, and don't forget to remind Hilda that we won't be dining in tonight."

Her eyes flashed, her body tensed. Morgan had seen the same thing happen when his sister, Sierra, became angry. The quiet before the storm. Morgan waited for Phoenix to tell the bossy Duval to take a flying leap. Instead, in the next breath, she seemed to retreat before his eyes, leaving only the façade and none of the brilliance of the vivacious woman who had entered the room. It was as if a shade had been placed over a bright flame. Again Morgan wondered what was the relationship between the two.

"Of course, Andre. Good-bye, Mr. Grayson."

"Good-bye, Phoenix," he said, unable to keep the disappointment out of his voice that she was leaving, and that she hadn't stood up to Duval. The door closed softly behind her.

"I'll show you out." Coming from around the desk, Andre led the way out of his study. As soon as they emerged, the same servant Morgan had seen earlier appeared. The elderly man reached the front door seconds before Duval stepped onto the terrazzo entryway. Despite the man's stiff left leg, Andre had not slowed in his haste to rid himself of Morgan.

Hands stuffed into the pockets of his jacket, Andre stood to the side as Morgan passed. "I'll mail the contracts directly back to Kenneth. There is no need to trouble yourself driving all the way back out here."

Morgan stopped in the middle of the stone walkway and turned. Duval wouldn't care if Morgan slow-roasted on a spit. They both knew it. He wondered why he even bothered to lie, and then he caught a movement . . . a flash of white behind him. *Phoenix.*

Inclining his head in acknowledgment, Morgan opened the car door, tossed his briefcase onto the passenger seat, then got in. Driving away, he again wondered exactly what the relationship was between Duval and Phoenix. Neither gave out signals of being lovers, but that didn't mean they hadn't been intimate.

Morgan might not like the snobbish man, but he was well-respected and wielded a great deal of influence in the art world. Certain women were attracted to that type of man. But for some odd reason Morgan didn't think Phoenix was that kind of woman. In his profession he had learned to read people quickly and accurately. Users weren't guileless and they certainly didn't blush.

Flipping on the signal, Morgan pulled onto the highway and headed back toward Santa Fe. He didn't like puzzles. He liked even less the pompous way Duval had treated Phoenix. Before the Roadster had gone another mile, Morgan knew he was going to find out exactly what was going on between the two.

"I thought I'd find you in here."

Phoenix turned from slipping on her smock to see Andre enter the studio. Bright sunlight streamed through the three floor-to-ceiling windows behind her. The rays weren't kind to Andre. They sought out every line in his sixty-two-year-old face, and delineated his thin frame. Unbidden came the contrasting and very vivid image of Morgan Grayson.

The moment she'd seen Andre's visitor, she had been captivated by the intensity of his gaze, his raw masculinity his expensive suit couldn't hide. There had been something untamed and noble about him. Instinctively she'd known he'd make a good friend or a dangerous enemy.

"You aren't annoyed with me, are you?" Andre persisted.

She took her time buttoning the faded smock. They both knew it wouldn't matter if she were, just as they both knew he wasn't going to change. He was an artistic genius with the temperament to match. He could be rude, harsh, insensitive, but she never forgot he had saved her when no one else had cared.

She took a seat at the stool in front of the workbench. "Why were you so abrupt with him?"

"He was sizing you up."

Phoenix blinked, then laughed despite the sudden pounding of her heart. "He was doing no such thing."

"You always think the best of people," Andre sneered, looking down his nose at her. "You believed the same of Paul Jovan."

Phoenix's entire body stiffened.

"I'm sorry you made it necessary to remind you of the incident," Andre said, his black-gloved hand sweeping over her hair. "Your naiveté and beauty attracts the wrong type of men. I'm the only man you can trust. Remember that." Without another word, Andre left the studio. There was no need for him to remain. He had accomplished what he'd intended.

Phoenix removed the cloth from the bust, lifted a pick, and began to delicately remove the excess clay. She couldn't argue even if she wanted to. Andre was right. He was the only man . . . including her father . . . who had ever wanted her for herself. She must not forget that ever again.